NIGHTMARE
TENANT

Paperback edition originally published March 2021; revised April 2021. Edition 1.1

KDP (Paperback edition) ISBN 9798728473244

Cover design by GermanCreative

Author photo by Mark Lever

Discover more of Richard Holliday's work at
richardholliday.co.uk

NIGHTMARE TENANT

RICHARD HOLLIDAY

PROLOGUE
THROUGH THE KEYHOLE

The halogen work light burned across the duty landing, surrounded by the gloom of a wintry evening. Motes of dust hung like fireflies in the harsh glare.

Jamie slurped on a pallid, lukewarm cup of tea as his mates swung their hammers at the brown concrete.

'Don't you sit there drinking a brew while we do all the hard work!' Jason, one of the other lads, breathed between swings. 'This shit's hard. And it was your idea to stay late!'

'Nah mate,' Jamie retorted, putting the chipped mug down. Jason paused, leaning the sledgehammer against the wall. Jamie approached. 'You three took too long fannying around at lunch.' Jamie reached for the sledgehammer. 'Come on then, give it here.'

'Have it, man,' Jason said. 'That shit's rock hard. Should've used the heavy metal.'

'Look,' Jamie gasped, pulling the hammer up with a swing. 'This is how you do it...'

The hammer came round like a pendulum, the head contacting the old blockwork with a booming thud that dislodged a cloud of ancient concrete dust. In the uneven light, it sparkled light blue before disappearing. The hammer fell to the floor with a metallic ting.

'See,' said Jamie, 'cracked it. Let's get it down then, once you break through it's easy!'

The lads picked up their sledgehammers with a renewed sense of purpose and eagerness. They'd been trying to get this wall down for the whole day. For most of the afternoon, the brick hadn't bowed, yet somehow, way past the normal clocking-off time, it decided to give in a cloud of dust.

'Whoever laid those bricks didn't intend 'em to come down ever again!' one of the others, Stevo, heaved. The wall quickly crumbled into ruins that piled at the foot of the gaping opening.

Behind the brick facade was torn, brown paper that hung off old sticky tape, ripped in places where the falling bricks and swinging hammerheads had nicked it.

'Well,' Nabil crowed, 'what's all that behind it?'

Jamie laughed, reaching out with a dusty hand to the paper, which gave no resistance to a firm tug. 'Let's pull it back and see?!'

The paper tore loudly and folded over the broken bricks. Stevo grabbed the work light and swung it round. It illuminated a series of cracked, glazed tiles in teal and white arranged in some geometric pattern, resembling stylised arrowheads. Wedges. Chevrons.

Nabil croaked. 'What was it the boss said about original features?'

Jamie scoffed. 'Look at it. They'll want to redo all this. Look, the tile is all cracked and filthy.'

'Are you sure that wasn't us?' Stevo ventured. 'You saw how much swing those bricks took.'

'Look, does it matter? Let's clean up and get out of here. We've done the day's work, we'll get paid tomorrow and it's a weekend with the missus for me.'

The four workers spent the next twenty minutes shovelling the broken brick and cement into a wheelbarrow. It would wait until the morning to go down the chute into the skip in the yard.

Stevo scraped his shovel into a pile of the rubble, picking the last of it up and swinging it with one motion toward the barrow.

'Wait!' Jamie said. Stevo stopped, the shovel hovering in mid-air.

'What?'

'Is there something in there?'

'Oh, come on, Jamie...'

Jamie knelt down and examined the shovel. His nose wrinkled and he stood back up, and nodded to the barrow. Eddie emptied the shovel with a rattle. 'Thought I saw something in there, something blue...'

'If it ain't lumps of gold,' Jason laughed, 'I'm not interested.'

'Come on then, lads,' Stevo said. He put the shovel down. 'Let's get down the pub! I'm gasping, and they're playing!'

Jamie laughed. 'Won't her indoors be up the wall if you don't get in.'

Stevo snorted with laughter. 'At you she will! As it was down to you! She knows better on a game night. Oh yeah, news for you Jamie boy - you're buying!'

Jamie laughed with the other guys as they trooped down the stairs. The worksite door squealed open in front and clattered shut behind. The banter was par for the course in this job.

Rounding through the gate at the perimeter of the site, Jamie took a glance up at the building. The tower should've been a black obelisk on the night sky. But he stopped - it wasn't. Not that night anyway.

The other guys stopped a few paces ahead.

Stevo turned. 'What now?'

'Did you turn the work light off?'

'Of course. Unplugged it from the transformer too. Like we do every night. Why'd ya...' Stevo trailed off, looking at the tower. There was a warm glow right at the very top.

'Are you sure?' Jamie asked.

'We were only on eleven, no way it should be on all the way up top,' Stevo said. 'Want me to go up there?'

'What?' Jamie said. 'Oh, no no. I'll go up. You guys, you get a table at the Arms.'

'Please!' Nabil shouted. 'Jamie's just trying to get out of buying the first round!'

Jamie rolled his eyes. 'Won't be long guys.'

'Alright,' Stevo said, and started to walk away, 'but don't be all night! Match starts soon!'

Jamie trotted through the gate. It wasn't locked. It never had been and was a world away from needing to be. Nobody had ever wanted to come here, not until the crews had arrived. Even then it was a building site. Rutted, muddy ground around the shell of a building. Looking up, Jamie felt that ominous, imposing presence even from the silhouette of the angular, cutting concrete. It was totally dark, but for the flicker of light from the very top, and a breath of cold swept down the very facade. Jamie quickly entered. He grabbed a torch from the equipment rack that was inside what would very soon be a plush lobby. Already the bones of the new life the tower was taking were being grafted into the original structure. Bolts with the new were driven resolutely into weary, brown concrete.

The light flashed across a multitude of unfinished surfaces and structures. Jamie walked past the lift, straight into the stairwell in the core of the building. 'Fucking lift,' he cursed, not relishing the jog up twenty-three stories of bare concrete steps. The lift hadn't yet been attended to. Not his job, Jamie thought, but it would save a lot of work when it was done.

His hefty boots clomped up the stairwell. It was a tough climb, Jamie's breath hoarse and laboured after a few minutes of solid ascent. His mind wandered - the others were likely already sipping the cool suds of their first beers. Maybe even their second. Maybe even United has scored, and they were celebrating. *Bastards.*

'That's weird,' Jamie mused to himself as he emerged onto the twenty-third floor. A piece of A4 paper hung where a pair of huge acrylic numerals would herald the floor number. It fluttered. He cast a glimpse around. There were no more stairs up. Wandering, the floor was totally empty, silent only for Jamie's boot thuds. It was totally dark too. He wandered around the stairwell, into the main hallway that led to the six flats on this floor. The doors were all absent; the flats were shells, soon to be transformed and sold for a pretty penny to those that fit the bill.

But there was still a draught. It came from upstairs.
But there wasn't an upstairs.
'Fuck it,' Jamie gasped in defeat. Turning, he went back

toward the stairwell. His face wrinkled at the prospect, though down had to be better than up.

Then the click came. Behind him. He shifted, just as the gust of cold, pallid air formed what felt like a vortex that surrounded him. He turned.

Whatever had done that wasn't there before. Jamie jogged around into the landing. The wind persisted. The builder followed it, rolling down his sleeves against the cold. The wind felt refrigerated, the hairs on Jamie's arms prickling under his overalls.

It was coming from behind the lift. Following the wind, which now howled and rattled a closed door, Jamie found the source. A maintenance cupboard whose door shivered against the jamb. Jamie opened the door, tugging at it at first. It didn't want to move initially, despite being loose in the frame. *It didn't want to be opened by him.*

He grunted, and the door lost, snapping open against the wall.

'Well blow me...' Jamie mouthed. The maintenance cupboard wasn't that at all; it housed a narrow, hidden spiral staircase. Led by his intrigue, and fuelled by guile, Jamie shone the torch upward and followed the cramped, narrow staircase up the dozen steps. Each step dislodged five decades of grime and grit. Jamie's breathing became shallow – his lungs averse to sucking in the ancient dust.

A solid wooden door greeted Jamie at the top of the clandestine stairs. He pushed on it. It didn't want to open, much like the lower door. But it gave to a concerted push.

Jamie nearly fell out of the opening into darkness. 'Holy Christ, what's that smell?!' he exclaimed. A palling, musky odour saturated the open space that the stairwell opened to. Looking out, Jamie saw plate glass on all sides, dirtied and tarnished by smears and moss. Beyond the glass was the night sky, and the lights of the city all around. But this space was black like the absolute darkness.

Jamie cast the torch around. There were shapes against the curtain-glass walls. Decrepit leather settees, threadbare and bald. Collapsing sideboards. Jamie hacked; the air was heavy with motes of dust, suspended in animation and almost time itself. The pile in the carpet was decayed, registering under his boots like a patchy and unmown lawn.

Clearly someone hadn't been here in a long time, and the world had forgotten about this place.

But around a corner, the lights were on.

'What the...' Jamie mouthed. He looked at the counter in the kitchenette. It was festooned with old, brown newspapers, dated from 1972, the year the tower was built.

Through a partition, Jamie found the source of the light in a room that housed a dishevelled bed, the covers falling apart and completely threadbare. Beyond the emaciated duvet, Jamie didn't bear to consider. The light showed the bedding to be rotten and discoloured by fluids of origins best left unknown.

Who would live in a house like this?

Jamie turned from the bedroom, shuffling quickly out. At the threshold of the concertina door that divided the space, he remembered: the lights! He reached in and felt for an antique light switch. His finger found it, but the switch lever was spongy and sticky. Peeking his head around, he saw the grime and grease that festooned the fitting.

'Fuck this, I'm outta-' he began, but was cut off by the *ping!* that came from a set of lift doors embedded into the wall. They were murky grey and tarnished. No light shone from them. He hadn't seen these as he had exited the stairwell. With a clank, the lift doors opened, and the tarnished chrome and dirty light of the lift car beckoned. Jamie found himself attracted, as if magnetically, to the lift.

'How...' he started. This didn't make sense. The lift didn't work. He remembered the breaker from downstairs, it wasn't just off, it was disconnected. There was no fuse. There was no way this could be powered. He'd climbed up those bloody stairs for nothing!

At the threshold, Jamie paused, then felt a shove. He fell into the lift. He reached for his shoulder, having felt the sensation of being pushed by something manifest and physical. Glancing over his shoulder, there was no-one there. Just the lights and stench of decades of decay.

'They can sod their electric bill, I need to get outta here!' he cursed. He reached for the button marked G on the panel. His finger closed the gap, but he withdrew it quickly with a yelp and a spark of static electricity. The doors closed in a thunderous clatter. A smoked-glass panel above the buttons illuminated.

However, the floor indicator wasn't a G, like Jamie expected, in a tarnished, faded lime green - he'd seen plenty of these in old Seventies lifts he'd ripped out before.

This one was claret red and flashed the letter B. For *Basement*.

'But there isn't a base-' Jamie mouthed, before the floor disappeared beneath his feet with a whoosh, and the lift descended into the depths, pulling Jamie with it.

ACT 1
VACANT POSSESSION

CHAPTER 1

FOUR MONTHS LATER

A streak of cloud smeared across an aquamarine sky. On an island on stilts in a sea of dark asphalt, the Mayor stepped onto a dais in front of an easy crowd. Behind him, suited dignitaries sitting on plastic chairs. They were all dressed smartly, clutching complimentary glasses of fizz that effervesced around the hubbub of conversation.

Behind, a gleaming new edifice stood where the dilapidated Tower once stood. In shiny, chrome letters, the name glistened.

CHIVRON TOWER

The Mayor tapped the microphone, emitting crackles of feedback. 'I declare,' he said with his chest puffed out, positing so the sunlight glinted off the ceremonial chain and robe, 'that this wonderfully-rejuvenated tower be open! Sandy,' the Mayor said to one of the people joining him on the stage, 'come and say a few words, this really has been a wonderful project, and we are so pleased you spearheaded the Borough Council into supporting it. Ladies and gentlemen,' the Mayor addressed, 'the chair of the Planning Committee!'

A nervous, crotchety figure toward the back of the stage fidgeted. Unlike the Mayor, who was filled out, this figure was pokey. Skittish. They flinched under the glare of attention. 'Thank you, Mr. Mayor,' the man, Councillor Sandy Grimms, grimaced through his rat-like features. 'If it's...'

'Councillor Grimms, please stop being so modest!' the Mayor

called again, with good humour but an intonation that it was no longer a request.

Rolling his eyes and trying to maintain a grin, Grimms took the microphone.

'Thank you, Mayor, for your introductions. And thanks to you all,' Grimms addressed the crowd, 'for attending this function. It was through tenacity and skill that the partnership between Borough Council and ambitious developers turned the Chivron Tower from the relic we all knew into homes for all our residents. Good homes. For good residents, yes.'

'Three cheers,' the Mayor called, taking the microphone back, 'to our fantastic task force!' The thinned-out crowd cheered and broke into scattered, well-meaning applause. A lady in the crowd gestured to a companion who held a camera on a strap around his neck. The shutter screeched. The Mayor pointed. 'It seems we have a member of the local press with us, to mark this-'

The woman swept her hair back and cupped her mouth. 'Mr. Mayor,' she hectored. 'What say you to rumours that the Tower was condemned back in-'

The Mayor waved with a Cheshire grin. 'You see behind you, the work we've done. Every inch of this impressive building has been-'

'Where did the money come from? What dirty deal did you and your predecessor do to secure-'

The Mayor looked nervous. The crowd had stopped clapping and chattering. Now they faced the woman, who stepped forward.

'Ms. Howes, yes?' the Mayor asked. 'With the Chronicle, isn't it?'

'Yes. We've spoken before. You remember, that builder that went missing. He was employed by the developers you so proudly chain yourself to.'

'Let me assure you that every single brick of this Tower has been rejuvenated by our talented team, and expertly overseen by Councillor Grimms and his committee and department.'

'You didn't answer about Mayor Stevenson, he had to-'

'Now, Ms. Howes,' the Mayor said. 'Let us not spoil this glorious day with that... *business*. The police found nothing. Not on Mayor Stevenson nor that unfortunate contractor. You *know* this.'

The reporter screwed her face. She indicated to her companion to turn and leave. The Mayor wasn't giving anything away. The casual chatter and hubbub that came with these sorts of things resumed to fill the car park.

Stepping down from the stage, Councillor Grimms took a hankie out of his jacket pocket. His tie was already undone by the time his shoes hit the paved ground from the wooden steps.

'Sandy, well done. I know it's not your strong point, public speaking,' a voice called from behind him. Sandy turned. His face screwed up.

'You're a twat, Bob, and I don't care what you're wearing.'

'That's no way to speak to the Mayor.'

Sandy retrieved a cigarette from a pocket in his jacket. It met his lips. 'When does this damn thing finish anyway?'

'Couple more hours,' the Mayor replied. He indicated to the back of the stage, behind a glossy hoarding. 'Are you worried?'

'Do I have reason to be?'

'Not at all, Sandy. Forget the theatrics. I'm impressed,' he said, the corner of his mouth rising.

'That reporter. She had some damn cheek. The licences...'

'She's just with the local rag. She couldn't pin what happened to Stevenson on us. As for the licences and the paperwork, you worry needlessly. No-one will have any reason to doubt them. As long as people live here,' the Mayor said, glimpsing up at the Tower's bulk, 'there won't be any trouble, especially for you and I.'

'And that builder...'

'What I said on stage was no lie, Sandy. He doesn't matter. What matters is we're here. It's all worked out.'

Sandy turned toward the parking spaces. The Mayoral limo sat pride of place in the lot. An aging Mercedes. 'Are you going to replace it then?'

The Mayor laughed once. 'Good heavens, no. Would you?'

Sandy finally smiled. 'Not one chance. There has to be some perks to this lousy number.'

'My boy,' the Mayor laughed, sipping from his flute of council-provided bubbly, 'you're learning fast.'

The shiny new front door on flat number forty-four pushed open, the draught excluder crackling with the movement.

'Well, Jules, it's finally ours. In you go, kids,' the man urged playfully. 'Go find your room, leave the big one for your mum and me!'

The two twins, black-haired babes Edward and Beth, hurried forward with squeals of delight.

Jules, their mother hesitated. She looked into the children's dad's eyes. He took her hand, squeezing.

'Come on then, Mrs. Barton,' he smiled. 'Let's make this house a home.'

Finally crossing the threshold, Jules let herself enjoy the moment. It was brief, as the sounds of this new chapter of their reality came back through the void in the form of two excitable twin children.

The boxes followed up the stairs. Burly removal men hissed and sighed with effort, but Joel Barton pitched in too. 'Careful,' he urged one of the movers with a box marked Fragile in red-and-white tape. 'Drop that and she'll kill me!'

The mover laughed once, shuffling off to add the box to the pile in the living room. Joel bounded down into the lobby. The space was bright and airy, the walls full of plate glass and modern, minimalistic features. Ahead of the stairwell was the main entrance to the Tower, and rooms either side filled out the bottom floor. On the left was the Chivron Tower Public Space.

People bustled about inside the space moving tables and chairs for the meet-and-greet that evening. Not quite there yet.

Joel walked fast, outside into the spring sunshine. Beside the tall white van that had contained the Bartons' entire domestic life was another car, just pulling up. The bumper was splashed with dried-on dirt and scuffs. It was packed in the back with bags and belongings. The door to this car opened just as Joel walked from under the canopy of the Tower into the sunshine. He stopped, watching an elderly Indian gentleman clamber out of the clapped-out car. The man winced in silent pain, feeling his hip. Then he staggered round the bonnet to the passenger side, to help an equally-elderly lady out and to her feet. The man looked over and made eye contact with Joel. He smiled gently. Joel came over.

'Hello,' Joel began. 'Are you moving in, too?'

'Yes, thank you,' the man said, not paying much attention to Joel. 'Come on, Gopi, dear,' he said to the woman, 'nearly there.' The man moved to the rear of the car, pushing a button. Nothing happened. He heaved as much as he could at the boot lid. It didn't want to move, despite the roughly-packed stuff pushing against the tarnished glass.

A mover emerged from the Tower and walked behind Joel, scowling.

'Yes, I'll be up in a min,' Joel said. He looked, unsure at first, before quickly jogging over to the man's car. 'Let me help you,' Joel said warmly, jiggling the boot button. It shuddered open. 'I'm Joel Barton, flat forty-four.'

'Thank you,' the man smiled, putting a hand out to Joel. He took it, shaking it heartily. 'I'm Partha Choudhury, this is my wife Gopi. Flat forty-four, you say?'

'That's right.'

'It's so nice to know we will have a kind young man as our neighbour!' the woman, Gopi, called. 'We're forty-three.'

'I'll tell the twins to keep the noise down then!'

21

Gopi laughed. 'That's kind. I'm sure your children are absolutely fine.'

'Is this all you have?' Joel asked. 'We've still got half a truckful, are you going to be okay to get it upstairs? You take the lift,' he said as the mover walked past with another box. 'My guys will have to use the stairs.'

The mover sighed.

Nearby the sound of a clattering, loud car engine and screeching tyres punched through the calm suburban hubbub. Loud music followed it like a bad smell.

'No,' Partha said ruefully. 'That sounds like our own pride and joy come to help his dear old parents into their new home...'

A younger man bounded out of the car, dressed almost dishevelled mix of baggy trousers and a hoodie. 'Hey ma, pa.' He turned to Joel. 'Hey. Who's you?'

Joel's eyes widened. 'Joel Barton, I'll be your parents' neighbour.'

'That's cool man,' the brash young man said. And said no more.

'Manners!' Gopi chastised. 'Mr. Barton, this is Rajat, our, er... *pride and joy.*'

'Nice to meet you,' Joel said. Rajat fidgeted.

'Let's get this stuff moved, man,' he said to his parents. 'Got bare tings to do, you hear me?!'

Joel exchanged a sceptical look with a bashful - likely ashamed - Gopi and Partha. 'It was nice to meet you all,' he said smoothly, before belatedly grabbing a box from the truck and resuming the task of hauling their life into their new home in the sky.

CHAPTER 2

'Hey Beth,' Edward said in a hoarse whisper across the room. 'Are you awake?'

From her bed opposite, the girl shuffled under the duvet. It was covered in cartoon horses. Ed's was covered in rocket-ships. A few tip-taps of pattering petite feet came nearer, bouncing off the new, smooth floor.

'I said, are you awake?!' Ed whispered again, louder. His whisper was greeted a few moments later by an unimpressed harumph.

'Go back to bed, Ed.'

'Can't. Can't sleep.'

'How?' Beth yawned. 'I was so tired. So thank you for making me not sleep either.'

'Want to do something cool?'

'Like what?'

'Let's go outside.'

'No.' She paused. 'What do you mean, *outside*?'

'The other floors. Bet there's tons of cool stuff in a place like this. Come on. Have you even looked yet?'

Beth shook her head under her duvet. Clearly this was to be a losing battle. She tossed the duvet aside. Her feet found the cool floor. She glanced at the digital clock on the table beside her bed, the power cord roughly strewn around. Something to be tidied in time once the unpacking started and the sorting began in earnest. 'It's one in the morning. And we'll get told off.'

'Well, it's happening now, come on!' Ed urged. 'Follow me.'

She did so, out of the bedroom and past the closed door where the deep snores of their parents rang hollow against bare walls.

Ed led his sister past the closed door where their parents snored, the sound softened by the thickness of the barrier. Their feet pit-pattered on the cool laminate.

'Shh!' he whispered.

'Sorry!' Beth mouthed back.

Ed indicated toward the living room. A shimmering, aquamarine glow crept from around the door, faintly, but enough to contrast against the total, unchanging darkness of the night that had filled the flat.

Beth was more excited now. He hadn't been making it up. She paced quicker, following her brother.

Ed pushed through the ajar door. Beth followed. Her mouth dropped. The vista from the picture windows was one of thin threads of aquamarine and turquoise descending down the tower, right in front of the windows. They threaded inside, around boxes and bags of belongings.

'Pretty cool, huh?' Ed huffed proudly.

'What is that?' his sister asked. 'No, don't!' she hissed as Ed strode forward toward the window. 'Ed, stop!'

'Wimp,' he retorted, waving an arm through one of the threads, which disappeared. It's harmless enough isn't it.'

Beth followed, her steps slow with reservation.

'Are you sure?'

'I'm not going to open the window.'

'Where's it coming from?'

'Must be upstairs.'

'How do you know?'

'I don't,' Ed said. 'Let's find out.'

Ed breezed past and out of the living room. He pulled the lever on the front door. It clicked, not loud, but loud enough to sound almost deafening in the dead of night.

'Shh!' Beth hushed. Ed smirked. The closed bedroom door next to theirs didn't move. Nothing changed. His parents were still sleeping quietly in their bed.

Outside the flat, the lobby was silent but bright, the safety lighting illuminating the fresh paint and unmarked walls. Ed scampered to the lift, pressing the button. Up above came the whirring of the mechanism.

'That's noisy,' Beth urged.

'Race you to the top then!' Ed said, blowing a raspberry. The lift door clicked open. It bathed the gloomy landing with cool electric light. They went in and glanced at the impressive column of shiny chrome buttons.

'Where do we go?' Beth asked.

'It's obvious isn't it?' her brother said, shaking his head. He reached right up to the button marked 23. 'Top floor. Must be!'

The lift door swished closed. The car rumbled ever so slightly before it started its ascent. It only took a minute, with an electronic *ping* that signalled its arrival.

The door opened to the sterile light of the Twenty-Third floor landing. The two children scampered out, and the door closed. There were no windows on the landing, just front doors to flats that were securely closed.

'Well, it's not up here, is it, Ed?' Beth pouted. Her brother pulled a face. 'Let's go back. I want to go back to bed.'

'Baby!' Ed cawed. He stopped at the sound of a wooden rattle. 'What was that?' he said to Beth. She now shivered and held her arms close to keep the heat in. 'And are you cold?'

'It's freezing, Ed!' she responded, just as the wind whistled through the landing.

The rattle came again, and it was nearby. Ed sprinted, past his sister and past the lift to a buttoned-down door that was festooned with peeling warning labels. Beth came to join. 'That door's closed, Ed, you can't go in there! It's not safe.'

The cupboard door disagreed. It rattled open. Before the eyes of the children were a dusty set of stairs that looked like they hadn't been climbed in a hundred years.

Which wasn't strictly true, but they didn't know that...

Descending through the blackness came more threads of aquamarine light. Following that, the muffled hum of strings and woodwind music. It sounded... *old.*

'Let's go, this must be where that music's coming from!' Ed called with excitement. 'Race ya, sis!'

Beth ran after him, but there was no chance of passing him on the taught, constricted spiral of concrete steps.

The stairs opened out into a dark space that was surrounded on two walls by plate glass. The music was gone from the moment Ed stepped onto the carpet outside the stairs. He ran up to the window, into a sunken area framed with old couches, finding it foggy and murky. He ran a finger down a coating of grime on the inside, leaving a smeary trail.

'Yuck!' Beth grimaced.

'Look,' Ed said, motioning with his head toward the night outside. 'It's the city.'

'Wow, we must be a hundred floors up!' Beth said.

'The lift only went to twenty-three?'

Beth looked at him seriously. 'What's one higher than twenty-three?'

'Twenty... four?'

'Right.'

'Wasn't twenty-three the top button though?'

'Yes...' Beth's mouth fell open.

The music started again, this time clearer. Both children turned on a moment. Light flooded from behind the lift into the darkness. Beth wanted to scream but didn't. Ed wanted to run away but didn't. He ran, regardless, toward the light which came around the cracks of a partition door...

'Gotcha!' he called, throwing the door open with a clatter of plastic sheets. But there was no-one there. 'Oh.'

A click came from behind them.

'Hey there, kids,' a groan came from behind. The two children turned, suddenly seeing the room before illuminated in yellow incandescence. The walls were panelled in ugly old wood, the carpet a dirty, patchy royal blue.

But besides that, the room was empty.

Immediately, Ed's confidence evaporated. 'Who said that?'

'I did,' the voice oozed. 'You coming to join my party? I thought you might be.'

'What happens if we don't want to?' Beth ventured.

The voice didn't answer, but the familiar *ping* of the lift did. Beth walked out of the dishevelled bedroom first, into the open space. Part of it was a living room, against the curtain windows, with horrendously ancient leather settees, the leather cracked and bare. In the corner a dusty, wooden television set. She glanced left. Two old lift doors beckoned - literally - opening and closing a few inches. As she gradually approached, the doors opened wider, the darkness of the shaft an intoxicating influence.

Beth stood on the threshold, the shaft doors fully agape.

'Don't do it!' Ed warned from behind.

Beth didn't hear or didn't listen - it was hard to tell which. She glanced up, putting her head past the metal maw of the lift shaft. The blackened metal bottom of the lift car was just above the opening. It jittered on its stays, and she snapped her head down.

At the bottom she saw the skeletal remains of a man, surrounded by tools that glimmered, in the limited light, a slick, dark red.

The lift car juddered again, this time once, but violently.

'If you're bad while living in my Tower, that's what happens! To *you*!' the voice hectored.

Finally, Beth screamed, and ran, with her brother, down the tiny spiral of concrete steps and into the twenty-third floor landing, but didn't stop, pulling on the stairwell door and running down, their feet clattering, right to the Twelfth floor.

Safety from the nightmare up there. Or was it down there?

The door to Flat forty-four opened under a trembling hand, trying to keep it as quiet as possible. It sucked back into its frame, again under trembling hands. Beth and Ed looked at each other and held themselves for comfort. After a long moment, the shivering stopped and they turned, eager to get back to bed. Quietly, they pit-patted back to their room.

Ed glanced right first, sure of what he would see. But he stopped.

Beth jostled into him. 'Shh!'

'Look!' Ed whispered.

'Oh, no.' Beth hissed.

Their parents' bedroom door wasn't closed. It was ajar, just enough.

But there weren't any lights on. Maybe, just maybe...

The two twins slipped as quiet as shadows back into their room and back under the warming safety of the covers. Both closed their eyes, shivering. The sleep poured over them. But it was a fidgeting, restless sleep that embraced the Barton twins, one that would rack them for hours until the sun shone on them, on their first morning in their new home. The morning arrived, pulling back the lids of the children's eyes with the warm rays of spring sunshine.

The bedroom door swung open. Their mum stood there, a hand still on the door.

'I'm glad you're both up,' she said neutrally, her voice without any warmth. This immediately prickled on the skin of the twins, who exchanged the briefest of brief glances. 'Come and have breakfast, and your dad and I will need to have a word.'

'About what,' Ed ventured with a yawn.

'Last night,' was all that their mum managed before sweeping the door closed again. It clicked shut.

Ed and Beth gulped. This was the worst part, and it didn't

happen often - the time between knowing they'd been found out, and the punishment.

Beth felt that feeling in the pit of her stomach, just like the feeling when she'd looked down the lift shaft. She swallowed hard.

They pulled socks on from boxes in the bedroom and opened the door, turning to face the music, but with their own story to tell too.

The twenty-third floor lobby beckoned, and the cupboard behind the lift held its secrets close.

Joel Barton eyed the hatch in the wall. He gave it another resolute press with his hand. It didn't move, not a millimetre.

'And you thought poking around in some utility closet in the middle of the night was a great idea?!'

'But Dad,' Ed protested, 'it *did* move! There's really some stairs up there, and some grotty flat, it looks over the city. And someone, I don't know *who*, but they *do*... lives there.'

'We'll see,' Joel said. He nodded to the stairwell door. 'Down, you two.'

'Can we not take the lift?'

Joel laughed. 'You wanted to show me some stairs, so show me the ones you're walking down back to the flat.'

Ed and Beth shrugged, defeated.

CHAPTER 3

'Thanks, Mr. Wentworth,' Joel said into his phone. 'I appreciate the update. Take care.' He hung up. Then he looked to his two waiting children.

'What did he say?' Beth asked.

'There's an old penthouse on the roof, yes, but there's no way up there. They're actually going to remove it in the summer, now you've mentioned it. They've had an offer of a mast on top of the tower, 5G, something nice and fast. So definitely, *definitely*,' he stressed, 'no playing up there even if you *did* find a way in.'

'But, Dad, you have to believe us...' Ed started, but was cut off when Jules, their mum, entered the lounge.

'That's enough, you two. I know it's all exciting exploring this new tower we live in but enough! You can't get to the penthouse, so don't be trying again! Maybe help you and your dad sort this place out so it's more like a home, don't you think? Starting, I think, with your room?'

The twins looked at each other, then back to Jules. 'Yes, mum.'

'We'll be good,' Beth said.

'That's better, now get back to unpacking. If you have it done nicely by tea we'll get pizza.'

The twins beamed at the notion of pizza and ran into their room in a flurry of excitement. The sound of boxes being torn open came through the wall, followed by the chatter and laughter of good children.

Joel and Jules made their way into the kitchen, still packed with boxes but some had disgorged their contents onto the countertops, now a collection of clutter, culpable to the cupboards.

'It's looking better in here already,' he said. Jules' face was ashen.

'Don't bullshit me.'

'What did I do?'

'You indulged them.'

'They're kids, we have to. Probably all sorts of nooks and crannies in this place to get lost in.'

'I care how we look here, Joel. Now it looks like we have nutty, out of control kids.'

'You know that's not true.'

'Isn't it? God, back when...' she trailed off. 'I thought this would be different, Joel. You *promised* me it would be different.'

'Honey,' Joel said, stepping closer. He put both hands on her shoulders. 'Kids being kids. They're our kids, and they're great kids. They won't be screwups, not like-'

'Don't even mention it!' she snapped, pulling back. 'I've... news.'

'Oh?'

'My parents...'

'Oh jeez.'

'They want to come and see our new place. The one they graciously put eighty grand into.'

Joel rolled his eyes. 'We're going to rue the day, you know that. When?'

'The weekend.'

'Next weekend?'

'Nope.'

'It's Thursday.'

'We'd better make this place look presentable, or they'll only make comments.'

Joel laughed. 'Your parents sure are funny.'

Jules looked at him severely but cracked a grin. 'They're bastards. And you're a bastard too, Joel Barton!'

'I know,' he smiled back. He leant forward, embracing his wife, and moving in for a kiss. 'Come here...'

Later, the twins fell into their now-tidy bedroom after a hearty meal of pizza. Ed climbed into his bed first. The bed was surrounded now by a conspicuously lower number of boxes. Beth climbed into her bed a moment later..

'Night kids,' Jules said warmly. 'Sleep well, and please, stay inside.'

'Yes, Mum,' Beth said. 'I'll be good.'

'That's nice. Otherwise, I'll tell Gran and Grandad.'

'Oh, no!' Ed gasped.

Jules left, closing the door with a gentle thud.

The children fidgeted in their beds.

'What time are mum and dad going to bed, do you think?' Ed said.

'You're not thinking of going out are you?!' his sister replied. 'You heard! And I don't want to go back up there, no way.'

'Typical girl, what a chicken!'

'Stop it, Ed!' Beth shouted.

From down the hall, their dad's voice hollered: 'That doesn't sound like sleeping in there!'

'Well,' Beth continued, quieter. 'I'm not going Ed. You didn't see what I saw. You're on your own. If you feel that brave.'

In the kitchen, the clink and clatter of crockery in the sink was followed by the jetting swoosh of water.

'That was nice,' Joel sighed. 'My compliments to the chef.'

'Papa John?!' Jules laughed.

'I'll check on the kids,' Joel said.

Jules nodded. 'I'll be along soon.'

Joel walked out of the living room and down the hall, toward the door to the children's room. It was closed, just as his wife had left it a couple of hours ago. He yawned, putting a hand on the handle, but quietly.

The door swung open ever so slightly, and Joel smiled. Both twins were snoozing, their faces restful and content, like a child's face should be as they slept.

Joel then closed the door as quietly as he'd opened it. Then he turned to the identical door in next to it. It opened, slightly less quietly, rubbing just a tiny bit on the carpet. He hummed. That'd need looking at.

Stripping off his T-shirt and jogging bottoms, he climbed into the king-size bed that was the sole defining feature in the room. Boxes and cases lined the walls. He looked at the lamp and alarm clock nestled on one such cardboard box, the red LED digits glowing onto his retinas.

23:46. A late night. But no work tomorrow.

Jules followed Joel into the bedroom. Like Joel, she quickly disrobed. Reaching for a pyjama set that lay loosely atop an open suitcase, she felt two hands on her waist. The fingers wandered.

'Don't bother,' Joel growled, pulling her onto the bed backwards. She giggled, landing on the duvet. 'You won't need 'em.'

CHAPTER 4

In the darkness, the twins snoozed.

Then, it came.

Muffled but distinct instrumental music, as if piped through a speaker right into the twins' room.

It was the same tired notes of woodwind and analogue synthesisers as before.

Ed got out of bed straight away, moving over to his sister. She was awake. She then frowned.

The music stopped as quickly as it had started.

Beth turned over in her bed, covering her head with her pillow.

The sickly voice from the penthouse licked, right into her ears. 'Don't be shy, little girl. Be good. Or be bad. I showed you what happens to those who are *bad*, didn't I?'

Beth shot up in her bed. 'Let's go,' she said to Ed. 'Now.'

'You sure? You were a scaredy-cat before.'

'That was when it was up there. Not down here.'

Ed opened the bedroom door and snuck out, wary for his parents. There were weird sounds coming from behind their bedroom door as he sidled past. It was securely closed, alright, but his mum seemed to be giggling here and there, and his dad grunting, like he was lifting heavy furniture.

That doesn't sound like sleeping in there...

'Get the door,' he hummed to Beth. She did so. The handle

rattled impotently in her hand. Ed rolled his eyes and pushed forward. The latch turned with a *thunk*. Then the Twelfth Floor landing greeted them, the stairway window a vista to the city in the distance.

They went straight for the lift, guided by that familiar sense of chill. It pulled at the little hairs on their skin. Then it swept them upstairs.

Behind the twins, though, the front door to Flat Forty-four fell open again, footsteps falling out and making for the stairs.

The lift ignored the Twenty-third floor landing, sweeping further upwards, and clattering to a resolute halt. The door opened, and the twins fell onto the filthy shag of the penthouse carpet.

The room was lit up in yellow electric light but devoid of life.

'Welcome, children!' the voice called, still bodiless. 'Welcome to my humble abode! Please, make yourself comfortable on my plush furnishings, all the rage, you know!'

Beth and Ed cast a risible glimpse at the decaying sofa. The leather was cracked and splitting. The ancient television, a grey glass screen encased in worn veneered wood, displayed only static.

A floor below, the stairwell door flung open, clattering. An instinct drew the pursuer to the cupboard behind the lift shaft. The panel behind the lift rattled, wanting to be found. It opened, and the pursuer went up the narrow, cloying stairway.

The door at the top flung open. The twins turned around, aghast.

'Dad, what are you doing here?!'

'I could ask...' Joel started, wearing nothing but a loosely fitting pair of pyjama bottoms. He breathed hard from the exertion, his body misted with a sheen of perspiration. His eyes widened. 'What the hell is this place?!'

'We don't know!' Beth called.

The lights of the penthouse burned brighter, pulsating in

brightness. The space was *affronted* by Joel's question, despite appearing to welcome him in.

'Downstairs, now, both of you!' Joel called, whisking the frightened children downstairs the way he'd came. 'I dunno what this is but *out!*'

Joel and the children bounded downstairs, all the way to Flat Forty-four eleven floors down. The wind followed them, pushing them away from the apparent source.

In minutes that felt like hours, they were back at the safe threshold of Flat Forty-four. The door slammed shut behind them.

'Go back to your room, kids,' Joel urged breathlessly, pushing the bedroom door open. He strode in, seeing Jules standing by the dresser, covered in her pyjamas.

'What was that?'

'They went upstairs.'

'Again?'

'So did I.'

'What, upstairs.'

'Yes.'

'To the Twenty-third Floor?'

'No. I went *upstairs*, Jules.'

'What's up from the Twenty-third?'

Joel sighed a great sigh and sat on the edge of the bed. 'Somehow, a Twenty-*fourth* Floor. That bloody penthouse.'

'And what is there that's got you so worked up?'

Joel sat on the edge of the bed and took a big breath. 'You ever... feel like something ain't right? There was a stink, like something was rotten. I... I can't put my finger on it.'

Jules said nothing for a moment. Then she cleared her throat. 'Okay.'

Joel turned to her. 'Okay?'

'You're drenched in sweat. Last time you were like this was when we decided-'

'Stop.'

She continued: '- to ask my parents-'

'Stop!' He said. 'But there's something up there. On Twenty-four. The roof. Penthouse. Whatever. It just felt like it shouldn't be there.'

'But that can't be, you read the brochure; that's impossible...'

'It's possible, alright,' Joel growled. 'And that Mr. Wentworth is going to hear all about this tomorrow. It needs bricking off.'

'Joel, come on, come to bed, whatever that was...' Jules urged, not sure what to say. She came around and sat next to Joel, embracing him. He held her too, not sure what to think, and fell into a restless, disjointed sleep.

CHAPTER 5

The next afternoon a slick, immaculate luxury sedan entered the estate, gliding to a smooth stop right outside the Tower. The driver walked toward the door - not far – with a swagger that belied his importance. He didn't glance at the building, not needing to take in its imposing stature. The angular outline demanded a casual glance from all that went to enter, crossing underneath the edifice into the entryway. He owned it, so he didn't need to observe it. It, instead, observed him.

The lift went *ping* on the Twelfth Floor. The suited man's hand rapped the composite door with definition. A few moments passed. It opened. The man faced an ashen-looking Joel Barton.

'Mr. Wentworth,' Joel said.

'Call me Dallas, my good man,' Wentworth said, holding out a hand. Joel eyed it for a second, then met the hand. The handshake was quickly over. Just a formality.

'Did you want to come in?'

'No, no,' Wentworth said. 'We had the formalities on the telephone, did we not?'

'We did, I suppose.'

'Show me what you found on the Twenty-third Floor.'

'Gladly.'

The pair took the lift. Joel and Dallas Wentworth said nothing to each other the whole way, which made the few minutes seem considerably longer.

Ping!

'Round here,' Joel said. Wentworth followed a few paces behind, taking airy strides behind the shuffle of the resident. His face twisted as the went round the back of the lift shaft and Joel pointed out the utility cupboard door.

'Are you sure, Mr. Barton, this is exactly where you found the...'

'Way up to the penthouse? Yes.'

'Fascinating,' Wentworth oozed. He gestured to the door, intending to touch it. His hand hovered. 'May I?'

'Knock yourself out.'

Wentworth shuffled, changing places in the tight space with Joel. 'You know, they say this Tower was Chivron's masterpiece. A symphony in concrete and steel.'

'Is that right? I thought it was a right dump before.'

Wentworth ignored the remark. 'We made that vision a reality at last. It was but an honour to work with the Borough to refurbish such a building to such high standards,' Wentworth continued. Joel carried on ignoring him. 'Huh,' Wentworth muttered. 'Panel does seem a little loose.'

'Can you get in?'

'Not sure,' Wentworth trailed off. His forehead contorted with effort as he rubbed the door with his hand. A few flecks of new paint fell onto Wentworth's suit. He brushed them off. Then he turned to Joel. 'Look, I'll get my builder here to take a look, as there's something not quite, well, right,' he breathed. 'We'll go behind the panel and see what's there. Brick it up. Make it look like it was never there. Would that satisfy you, Mr. Barton?'

Joel nodded. 'That would.'

'I'm glad it does.'

'Good, well don't let me keep you.'

Joel walked back around toward the lift. The lift door opened and closed with a clatter, the car rumbling gently as it descended.

Wentworth put a hand into his jacket pocket, pulling out his mobile phone. His fingers swished on the glass screen in furtive motions. Then he held up the phone. A second passed. He spoke without pleasantries. 'Mike. I'm here. Spoken to the guy. You know, the one I emailed you about. Found his dipshit kids *in the penthouse*,' Wentworth said in a mocking tone. 'I told you to get this thing *sorted*, buddy, so get it done,' he continued, feeling the ice-cold handle again. The door rattled, and Wentworth withdrew his hand in apparent horror. The door fell open. 'Gotta go. I think there is some truth to this. I'll get photos for you. I'll call you back.' Wentworth hung up but didn't pocket the phone; instead, he flicked a few more times on the screen and a pimple of bright white light blossomed from the rear. It illuminated a worn concrete step, curving around. He took a step, and another, letting the cloying space consume him as he followed the trail.

The flashlight on his phone shone against the walls. Old concrete, festooned with filth swallowed all the light from the camera.

'Huh.'

Wentworth took the first step. Then another. Going up.

The stairwell opened out into the open-plan space of the penthouse. Wentworth stopped on the threshold, where the staircase that didn't exist on paper exited into reality.

Wentworth tiptoed forward. The floor was mushy, the carpet the consistency of wild moss. He looked through the filthy, green-encrusted windows of the penthouse, over the modern City that sprouted from the horizon. Wentworth turned around, going through a doorway to the right. This led to a corridor. An open door called him forward. He walked toward it, poking his head into a decrepit bedroom. That was darkness, and he ignored it.

Then he passed a galley kitchen on the other side of an opening, littered with remnants of old food nibbled by vermin around ancient appliances. Past that, another room filled with a desk and rolls of paper around a large Formica table covered with rough drawings, pictures and technical diagrams.

Above the drafting table, a shelf with a collection of bound books. The subjects and titles seemed oddly familiar. The Smithsons. Goldfinger. Lasdun. A folder full of pieces about le Corbusier. Dallas picked up one of the loose sheets. He laughed at some of the phrasing. *Streets in the sky.* 'No money in that,' he said to himself. He recalled a site visit to the decrepit Tower with his architects, mapping out in white spray-paint where square-footage could be increased, reducing streets in the sky to alleyways in the angels.

Putting down the file, he moved sideways. He'd been in rooms like this before, recently when the Tower's rebirth was but a figment of his imagination. He recalled the meetings in snazzy, modern conference rooms, glossing over plans and ideas with his *architects*. He stopped smiling. It was no bedroom, but an office. Wentworth entered, looking at the documents. *Plans.*

'Good god...' he whispered. He picked up some of the dried-out paper. 'The plans for the Tower.' He thumbed through some of the other papers that littered the room. Designers for murals, details on the penthouse itself, original artists impressions of the impressive Tower as a beacon among a manicured, sparse garden. Streaks of clean off-white and wheatfield brown, stark against an imagined, watercolour sky. Then some paperwork specifying concrete finishes, the final approved choice being a brown pebble-stone that Wentworth had strove to eradicate in his makeover.

These documents represented the aspects of the Tower he had thrown away - that had made it the blot on the landscape that just wouldn't shift. The murals took his interest the most; he held one up, closely, under the crackling incandescent light. Plans for tiled murals on every landing, each a different variation of the same basic pattern - geometric arrows. *Chevrons.*

'That is how the Tower should always have looked,' a voice said from behind. The lights in the room erupted with a *fzzt* of current. Wentworth turned, expecting to see a figure in the doorway. But there was nobody there. 'And you, Dallas Wentworth, have defiled my creation?' The voice continued, as if it *were* there, right next to him.

'Your creation?' Wentworth gasped. 'Who the hell are you?'

'My name is on the Tower. You left that, at least.'

'What Tower?! This?! Oh. I see. This can't be real. You can't be... they said you...'

'Disappeared,' the voice said. Wentworth dropped the pieces of paper he still clutched. 'Oh please, I'm hardly going to harm you, not like this anyway. I will ask you some questions, though. Don't go, there's nothing to be *frightened* of.'

'Look, wherever it is you are, Halloween isn't for months. Are you a student? Is this some kind of prank. Not like we'd let that lot into the Tower, that'd cost too much to clean up.'

'I didn't build the Tower for you to make money!' the voice barked. 'Sit down for God's sake.' Dallas did so. The voice continued: 'It embodied a vision, and it's not whatever you or those you connived with think of it!'

Wentworth shook his head. 'Look, whoever you are, did you scare those poxy kids from Forty-four? And anyway, it's been agreed, the Tower will be quality housing. At long last.'

Silence.

'Who *are* you, anyway? Really? Not just some punk kid with a Bluetooth speaker.'

The voice gave a single laugh, attenuated through the crusty lightbulb. 'I'm the Architect. This is my life's work.'

'The Architect? Nah, I did my reading. Herve Chivron dis...' Wentworth trailed off. It clicked.

'Maybe you and I will meet soon, Dallas Wentworth. Maybe we will. Let's see, eh.'

The lights burned out with a crackle, leaving Dallas Wentworth sitting in the dark study of a man who should be dead.

He laughed. There was no other way to rationalise it. He

got up, dusting himself down. His suit jacket was covered in a layer of filthy cobwebs which settled into the stale air. Briskly he walked out.

Re-entering the living room, he regarded the space, mentally picturing what he *could* do with it. A gust of stale air from *somewhere* pushed him toward the doorway. From there, the little spiral staircase led back to civilisation on the Twenty-third floor. Wentworth turned, just seeing the maintenance panel snap shut.

Reaching into his pocket he pulled out his phone. It erupted with tinny obviously-fake shutter sounds.

'Mike. There's a wall I want built, up on the Twenty-three, and I want it built. There's something here I don't want to hear about again. Was it on the plans? Maybe I'll explain it sometime. But for now, I want a wall. I'll send you a pic, but get it done and I'll pay you triple.'

A flatbed truck pulled into the mostly-empty car park, next to the plush limousine that stood closes to the very entrance. The rough judder of the diesel engine serrated against the evening crimson.

Three guys bailed from the cab and pulled supplies from the truck.

They met a man outside, exchanged a few cursive glances and parted.

Joel emerged outside of his flat to the sound of builders trooping up the stairs, carrying bags of cement.

'What's going on?'

'We're building a wall?'

'Where?'

'Twenty-third Floor.'

'Why?'

'It's all here,' the builder said, thrusting a leaflet into Joel's hands. Turning and closing the door, Joel read the leaflet, now it was slightly crumpled:

**EFFECTIVE IMMEDIATELY, THE TWENTY THIRD FLOOR
IS OUT OF BOUNDS TO RESIDENTS OF CHIVRON TOWER
FOR REMEDIAL WORK. DO NOT ACCESS THIS FLOOR
UNDER ANY CIRCUMSTANCES.**

HOOK & LAY PROPERTY DEVELOPMENT LTD

'Sucks for whoever lives up there,' Joel hummed, closing the door on flat Forty-four. It was nearly teatime.

Outside, an engine turned over, and Dallas Wentworth skidded out of the car park without a glance back at his possession.

ACT 2
OWNER OCCUPIED

CHAPTER 6

Spring turned into a glorious summer that year. As the weeks passed with the evenings drawing longer, the Tower began to fill, from the bottom up. *Literally*.

Jules Barton was washing the dishes, like she did every evening, feeling the warm soapy water over her smooth hands. She hummed to no particular tune, the sounds of the television in the lounge muffled by the solid walls.

That suburban peace was shattered with the screams of some kind of social banshee from outside.

'You know what, TJ, you can really stick it up your arse for all I care!' a voice, ostensibly female, hectored into the evening twilight.

'Oh, that's your answer isn't it, Krystal - to 'stick it up your arse'. Well, *you* can stick it right up there, you talk out of it already!' a man yelled in a commoner's dialect.

Jules let the plate she was washing fall to the bottom of the sud-filled sink. Turning, she looked through the window in the kitchen, just about able to see downstairs. The shouting continued, followed by the staccato barking of an unattractive mutt.

Jules rolled her eyes and left the kitchen through the doorless archway to the lounge. Joel and the twins were watching the television. Her derisive glare caught his eyes.

'What's up?' he said, then muted the television. 'Oh. Again?'

'Fourth night this week,' Jules gesticulated. 'Wouldn't mind but they've only been here a couple of weeks!' She went to grab her jacket from the arm of an adjacent chair.

'Jules, don't,' Joel urged, reaching out in protest from the settee.

'No, I'm not having it, Joel,' she insisted, pulling the jacket on. 'She's not the only one who lives in this block...'

The front door clicked closed. Jules paced down the stairs. She didn't take the lift. The walk helped stir up her courage.

A few minutes of furtive tapping passed. The stairwell to the rest of the Tower opened onto the Second Floor landing. There she saw the piles of rubbish and broken bottles outside one of the newly occupied flats. But it got worse a few floors up. On the Fifth floor, outside flat Fifteen, the rubbish piled nearly to the letterbox. The other flats weren't much better, but it didn't take a genius to work out which flat was Krystal's. Jules thought of rapping on their door, demanding they button it. The shouting was carrying on outside. They weren't in. She nipped down the stairs into the lobby and then outside.

Both Krystal and TJ, her on-off boyfriend, continued arguing in inane and nonsensical non-sequiturs that made no sense to even the lowest of decent people. They continued, their language mindless, boorish and crude.

'Will you two, please, *shut the hell up*!' Jules bellowed from the doorway.

Krystal scowled, pausing her verbal tirade for the briefest of moments. She turned her head, her hair in plaits, and the electric light of the lamp-posts reflecting off her gaudy earrings. 'Mind your own, stupid cow,' she spat.

'What did you say?'

Krystal turned fully to face Jules in the shadow of the Tower. 'I said,' she spat again, 'mind your own, you stupid - *little* - cow.'

Jules' mouth fell agape. 'How dare you. Why don't you, your gob's been open more this last week...'

'Oh, shut up, I don't care!' Krystal sneered. 'This ain't nuthin' to do with you, is it?'

'I live here, it's absolutely something to do with me. All I have to listen to is you every evening. My kids have to listen! And you,' Jules said, casting a glimpse at the boyfriend. 'Whoever you are, you make it worse.'

'How?' TJ said. 'This is a private conversation, what are you getting your knickers wet over anyway.' He looked to Krystal. 'See, look what *you* did now, just because-'

'*Shut up already!*' Jules shouted again.

'Fuck! Off!' both Krystal and TJ responded.

'Do we *all* have to listen to this? Jeez, it's ridiculous!' Jules said. 'Can we go one week without you two kicking off about whatever it is you argue about?!'

Krystal pouted. 'Why, not much you can do now, is there? Stupid bitch, probably got a melon stuck in your crack, why're you mouthing off at me...'

Jules internally admitted she had a point. But she wasn't going to relinquish now. 'I'll get onto the Council in the morning! Start as you mean to go on.' Krystal laughed.

'They won't do nothin." TJ smirked. He pulled on the chain the big, ugly dog was on. It growled. 'Some prick with a clipboard doesn't scare me.'

'I'll do it!' Jules pointed.

'Look, lady,' TJ said, swaggering over. He took a big puff of the cannabis joint that wiggled between his fingers. He blew it harshly into Jules' face. 'I know people, right, that'd turn this place up, *ting*. You get me?'

Jules didn't. She didn't know what *up ting* even was. She just coughed away the stench of the weed.

'I'm just, well,' Jules stammered. 'Just saying, is all. There are other people living-'

'They ain't down here makin' a scene,' TJ growled. 'They're clever. They know to just shut their windows and let things be.' Krystal came over, tugging on TJ's arm. 'See, things resolve themselves proper good, right *ting*. So take yourself up those stairs,' he continued, making a stair-climbing gesture with two fingers, 'and don't be dissing me or my woman again. I don't even wanna *see* you, bitch. Now get out of my sight, right.'

Jules withdrew, back inside. She'd lost her head of steam completely. Laughing, Krystal and TJ followed, into flat Fifteen.

That show of force wasn't just for that crank, they thought. The whole Tower had heard that. Curtains had twitched. They'd be left to fester in their own mess now, and that was just how they liked it.

The next weekend, Jules found herself interrupted by a rapping on the door. She tutted, pulling a cardigan on as she reached for the door handle. It clicked, descended and pulled forward under her grip.

'Oh, Mrs. Barton,' Gopi Choudhury gasped with relief. 'I'm so glad someone was in!'

'What's happened?' Jules asked.

'Partha... Mr. Choudhury, my husband, he's in all sorts of trouble!'

'Trouble?! What trouble. Look,' Jules urged, 'lead the way. I'll try to help.'

They moved quickly over to the lift, Jules hammering the button. For a few seconds, nothing happened.

'Again?!' she cursed. 'Sorry, Mrs. Choudhury, we'll have to take the stairs.'

Mrs. Choudhury shrugged and shuffled across the landing.

Jules followed the little Indian lady down the stairwell, gasping for breath as they descended.

'It's those no-goods down below,' Gopi Choudhury sneered. 'Driving my husband nuts.'

'On the Fifth-'

'No,' Gopi urged. 'Not the Fifth floor. One above. The trouble

52

is getting closer and closer!'

'Really? I thought only nice people lived here.'

'So did I, but you've seen the new arrivals, yes?'

Jules grimaced, remembering her encounter with Krystal and her boyfriend. Indeed, the other residents that had moved in on opening had withdrawn into their flats. Only the brash recent arrivals from made their presence known.

They emerged onto the Sixth Floor landing.

Already the problem was evident. Loud, obnoxious bass music was erupting from a front door propped open by a rag-tag assortment of rucksacks and bags.

'Hello?' Jules ventured, poking her head into the flat. Gopi went to follow, but Jules held out a hand to hold her back.

The flat seemed empty. Jules found most of the rooms empty of furnishings but instead littered with random bags, rubbish and clutter of indeterminate origin.

'Who're you then?' a voice slurred. Jules pivoted. She was eye-to-eye with a zombie that swayed back and forth in a non-existent breeze.

'Er.' Jules stammered.

'That's him!' Gopi brayed. 'That's one of them! You fiend! You've done goodness-knows-what with my husband!'

'Hey, listen,' the figure slurred. It was human then. He stopped just long enough to swig from a can of beer that hung loosely in his grip. 'We're just here to have a good time, is all- hey wait, you said he's your husband?'

'Kai!' another voice called, and the bathroom door swung open. 'I don't think it's a costume, I think he's *actually* some Indian geezer. Proper corner-shop stuff. Oh,' the second figure murmured. 'You guys ain't-'

'Where is he?' Gopi bellowed, pushing her way past the two drunken figures and into the bathroom. 'Oh, Partha, goodness me!'

Jules followed with a severe look on her face. She found Gopi soothing her husband, who sat upright in the bath, the hose of the shower dangling in the tub, dancing like a fitful snake. She turned, toward the two figures who gave her wide-eyed, vacant looks, and clung onto only one thing: their booze.

'Do you two want to actually explain?'

'We thought he was here for the party,' the male figure burped.

'What party?'

'This party,' the female figure croaked.

'What a state to be in! You know there's kids here! And who are you, anyway?'

'Me?' the male figure sniffed. 'I'm Kai, that's my sis, Yanis.'

'Yanis,' Jules repeated. 'So, do you, actually live here?'

'Moved in last week! See, my parents, they got to this narky stage where they *couldn't handle us*,' Yanis said, making mocking quote gestures with her fingers.

'How charitable of them,' Jules said. 'Look, fair enough, but do you have to live like such absolute pigs?'

'We live how we live, man,' Kai swaggered. 'Anyway, can you lot, like, bounce now?'

Jules' eyes widened. 'Excuse me?'

'We've invited a load of, like, mates of ours, they're bringing some, like, *banging* tunes and whatnot.'

From inside the bathroom, the sound of splashing water had ceased, replaced by grunts of effort. Jules poked her head in once more, and saw Gopi struggling to pull her husband from the bath.

'Here, let me help!' Jules urged, helping to pull the man up and over the ledge of the bath. He was dripping with cold water, his clothes sodden and dark with the dampness.

Outside in the hallway and beyond, giggling and belching. The music started again.

Jules scowled. 'Stupid kids...'

'Come, Partha, we'll soon have you out and back...'

The bathroom door flung open. Kai stumbled in, his mostly-empty can leaking from its inversion in his bony grip.

'Outta the way!' he yelped, tumbling past Mr. Choudhury and falling over the edge of the bath. Then, loudly, he retched, vomiting a putrid pool of drink and stomach juices into the bath. The small bathroom, windowless, was quickly heaving with the stench.

Jules and the Choudhurys quickly vacated, retreating to the relative pleasantness of the Fifth Floor landing. Jules went to call the lift, leaving Gopi to comfort a shivering Mr. Choudhury.

The doors to the lift rumbled and vibrated. *Odd*, Jules thought. *I thought it wasn't working.*

The lift door went *ping*, and opened, releasing a group of twelve or so rowdy youths, giggling and braying like hyenas. They laughed, dancing around Jules and the Choudhurys, who tried to meander through the din and cheering youths. The noise increased tremendously. The group from the lift funnelled through the front door.

The cheers stopped in an instant though when a voice bellowed like a gunshot: '*Rajat!*'

Everyone froze on the spot, no longer jubilant or celebratory, with the music from the living room blasting impotently.

One member of the group from the lift shivered sheepishly. The crowd parted, leaving a lone, bashful figure in the middle of the landing.

'Hi, mum...' the figure mumbled.

'Are these friends of yours?!' Gopi said. 'Oh, you continue to *disappoint* me. Why?!'

Rajat shuffled.

Mrs. Choudhury snapped. 'Answer your mother! You think you will be attending this party now?! Look,' she gestured, her voice like a thundercrack, 'look what they did to your father!'

Rajat looked. Mr. Choudhury shivered, sodden. Father and son's eyes met at last, and Rajat knew that look. Mr. Choudhury's mouth turned at the lip, the bags under his eyes heavy with disappointment.

Jules could only observe, and realised that this was not the first time, and nor would it be the last time.

Eventually, the impact of Gopi's thundercrack mellowed and waned, the party atmosphere as intoxicating as the drink and booze itself. The door thudded shut, reducing the music and hubbub to muffled indistinction.

Gopi and her husband shuffled into the lift. Jules was the last to enter, but looked over, into the landing.

Rajat stood there, lost.

The lift doors started to clatter closed.

Jules met Rajat's lost gaze.

'I suggest you think about what matters,' she said.

Rajat stood, his eyes to the floor. A moment passed. He raised them. He stepped forward, toward the lift, but the doors closed. Jules made no attempt to stop them, instead remaining still.

The young man, brash in his appearance but shaken by the experience, trudged toward the stairwell.

They wouldn't forget this.

CHAPTER 7

With transition of seasons from summer to autumn, the temperature dropped. The playground outside Chivron Tower frosted over. Morning dew crystallising into beads of frost on the poles of the play equipment.

Inside the flats, life continued as it had done - without major incident. The Tower had, over that time, gradually and steadily filled like a vat. People shuffled in and out, the car park filling each evening, emptying the next morning. The stairwells thrummed with footsteps going up and down.

Toward the upper floors, blissful silence.

Unfortunately, it seemed, the grit and gristle filtered inexorably to the bottom.

Most evenings the Tower blazed with light, the tungsten and halogen glow irradiating against the night.

And life continued.

A few empty flats remained by October. These were steadily eaten by those seeking shelter from the cold and blustery winds, with nowhere else to go.

One evening that month, such a feast of vacant property took place. The sounds of moving in were not unusual by this point. Veteran residents - the Bartons, the Choudhurys and the residents above such as the Durands, Crombies and Townsleys, let the sounds mellow into ambience.

Near the top though, people shuffled, though the Bartons

never knew who lived up there. As those above the Bartons kept themselves to themselves more and more, those below made their presence known to an increasing degree, their lives, messy and unkempt, and unable to be confined to the walls of their flats.

Below the Bartons, lived the trouble, and above, lived those aspiring to more in life. The sort of people who'd drive an Audi to Joel Barton's Ford Mondeo. Below were the Nissan Micra crowd. Joel Barton rarely saw them but for more than a stolen moment in the mornings as they headed to their respective cars, parked opposite each other in the car park.

The separation, Joel had begun to think, was emblematic. The higher in the building you lived, the easier life seemed to be. Joel and his family were stuck in an urban purgatory.

The building, however, seemed to gradually settle, both into its existence and, with a few cracks, into its foundations. These were repaired, though the patches the decorators applied never *quite* matched.

One night, in the depths of slumber, Joel Barton was woken by the sensation of pulling on his face. He opened his eyes, and as his vision adapted, he saw the dewey-eyed face of his daughter, lip trembling.

'Daddy, there's a noise,' Beth moaned.

Joel yawned. He glanced at the digital clock. 'It's 3:15, honey. What noise? Did you wake your brother?'

'There's men, too. Outside. Downstairs. Doing something.'

Joel sighed, admitting defeat. The duvet fell away. Joel stepped out of the parental bedroom into the pitch-black hall. Beth had disappeared, but not into her bedroom, but toward the living room at the far end of the flat.

Joel followed. He heard a rattle. He stepped forward, the noise getting louder and more prominent with each step. The noise sounded like an engine, propelled into the flat on the wind. The breeze caught Joel's arms, prickling his skin. He entered the living room. He took a quick and deep intake of cold breath. The windows were all open, the blinds rattling against the walls.

'Did you open the windows?' he asked.

Beth shook her head. 'Nope, wasn't me.'

'I was sure they were closed when we went to bed,' he trailed off. 'Show me, then.'

Beth beckoned over to the window on the corner of the flat. These windows were the full height of the building, bisected horizontally into a top, glass section and a lower opaque piece. The top portion could tilt open. Joel glanced down, toward the asphalt lake at the base of the Tower.

There was an old, clapped-out van, and some men forming a counsel around the opened side doors.

Joel watched. Beth tugged on his pyjama bottoms.

'Go back to bed, sweetie,' he said to Beth, not taking his eyes off below. 'You'll be alright.'

Beth paddled off to her warm bed. Joel, however, stood at the window, watching the men. Quickly he dashed back to his bedroom, grabbed his phone and went back to the corner window, clasping the device.

'Oi Royston, hurry up with that, will ya?' one of the men called toward the tower entrance, his words forming clouds of breath that hung in the air.

'Button it, Surly,' another man said. 'Don't wake up the neighbourhood!

The third man snorted and rubbed his gloved hands. 'Quiet. He'll be here. He always delivers the goods.'

A door clicked. From the gloom a heavy, wide figure emerged clutching two full-looking black binbags. Surly smiled.

'Pleasure doin' business with-'

'Hey, hey!' Royston hushed. 'I'm just takin' out my rubbish, and you fine gentlemen, you're just my binmen.' Royston nodded to the van. 'The bin lorry looks the part, I will attest.'

Surly opened one of the binbags and held it to his face.

He inhaled, deeply, his face emerging with a contented smile illuminated by the street lights. His eyes rolled in pleasure, but they came down and Surly's face hardened.

His eyes darted upward, toward the Tower. Toward a window. Was that a figure?

Who was up there watching?

Joel ducked away from the window. He breathed hard.

With tiny movements, his curiosity drew him back to the glass.

'Come on, Surly, whatcha even looking at?' one of the men asked.

'I thought I saw someone in the window?'

Royston turned and gave the Tower the most cursory of glances. 'They're all sleeping. Now,' he turned to Surly, 'there's the matter of my payment.'

'Never a dull moment with you, Royston.'

'Come on, man. We've done this before. New home, same game, isn't it?'

Surly looked at the tower for a few more moments. Then he focused. He put his dirty hands into his faded, worn jeans and pulled from the pocket cash, with fronds of loose tobacco among the notes. He shoved them into Royston's grubby mitt.

'This ain't the usual venue,' Surly burbled.

'It was a steal. Nobody'll think to look at this brand new pad.'

Surly hummed. The moonlight glinted off the chrome lettering. 'True. Now go.'

'A pleasure,' Royston said. No more words were exchanged. Surly and his two lackeys climbed into the van and drove off, the engine rattling into the distance. Royston stayed outside, thumbing through the notes. He smiled, laughing just enough that he could hear.

Royston jogged back into the ground floor entrance hall.

He ducked to the right and produced a key from his tracksuit pocket. The mechanical room door opened with a click, with a steady, loud electrical hum emitting into the dark lobby.

With a single chuckle, he stuck his head in and retreated, locking the door once more. He went up, calling the lift.

Two figures loomed in the darkness, silently watching Royston, and then let themselves into the mechanical room, drawn toward the steady buzzing.

Whoever they were, they knew what he was up to.

CHAPTER 8

The aluminium letter flap to the door of Flat forty-four rattled. A handful of envelopes dropped onto the doormat just inside.

It was a Saturday, so everyone was home.

'Dad!' Ed called to his father. 'Post!'

Joel emerged and took the pile of envelopes from his son. He quickly discarded three: they were circulars, addressed to 'legal occupiers' and 'residents'. These were names that Joel never answered to.

But a thicker envelope aroused some intrigue. Joel ran a finger inside the edge of the flap, tearing it roughly with a staccato ripping. He unfolded the paper within. He recognised the logo: a modern, soulless and shapeless interpretation of an incandescent bulb favoured by the utility company.

What the letter said, though, was as foreign to Joel as a Swahili dictionary.

'Hey, Jules!' he called, getting up and moving into the kitchen. 'Jules,' he said as he met eyes with his wife, 'look at this.'

She took the letter and laughed almost immediately. 'That can't be real.'

'Eight-hundred and seventy-nine pounds for electricity? In a month?' Joel glanced out of the kitchen. 'No, I can't see any floodlights in there. Say, where are you hiding the twenty toasters you've clearly got going...'

'Funny,' she said. 'That must be a typo, what was it last month?' Jules asked, going with Joel into the lounge. There he dug around in a box of paperwork. He unclipped a similarly-printed bill with the same logo as the one Jules held.

'There, we paid fifty-six seventy. And even I thought that was a bit steep. LED bulbs everywhere!'

'Phone them, that's not right. And we're definitely not paying it!'

'Damn right,' Joel said, picking up his mobile and keying in the customer service number from the letter. He navigated - painfully - the telephone prompts. Finally, he clicked through to a human agent, casually forgetting the name of them the second they offered it to him.

The conversation lasted only a few minutes. Jules looked across from the door to the hall.

'It's all legit,' Joel sighed. 'The meter readings are taken remotely, on one of those smart meters. All standard these days.'

'My parents still won't have one, they see it as all-'

'Yes, well,' Joel cut in, 'we know what your parents are like.'

'My parents?!'

'Yes, your parents. *Anyway,*' he sucked through his teeth, 'any issues should go to the building manager. Who you may recall, I've met.'

'That Mr. Wentworth, wasn't it?'

'Are you going to call him?'

'Not immediately, no.'

'But Joel, it's-'

'And no,' he said, getting up and opening a closet built into the lounge wall. 'Don't call *your parents* either.'

'I wasn't going to!'

'You're already reaching for your phone, Jules.'

'I thought it went off.'

'It didn't.'

'Well, mum usually calls anyway, you know what-'

'Enough,' Joel said. He pulled himself out of the cupboard holding a small torch and a screwdriver. Then he turned, going past his wife and toward the threshold of the front door. The latch clicked.

'Where are you going?' she asked.

'Just downstairs, to look at the fuse board. Check the meter. This,' he waved the bill, 'ain't right.'

'Is that a good idea?'

'We'll see. Won't be long.' Joel said, letting the door close. He called the lift and selected from the button for the ground floor. The lift shuddered, acquiescing to his request with a muted clatter of the doors closing. Then the motion started.

He whistled, in absence of any other tune.

The door complained and opened quickly once the lift stopped. Clearly it wanted Joel's tuneless whistling out.

The entrance lobby was empty, and Joel swept toward the mechanical room. The door sprung open as he approached, the latch popping out of the frame.

Weird.

Joel followed the loud humming into the mechanical room. There he ducked around some ducting until he was confronted with the utility cupboard, whose door looked distinctly *original* to the building.

The danger signs on the utility cabinet doors beckoned. The cupboard door scuffed the bare concrete. Then, with a squeal, the metal door to the main fuse cabinet opened.

'Huh,' Joel coughed. From the ground came an obviously-old cable, the sheathing a little frayed and coated with dust. The rest of the fuse board was a mishmash of old equipment with modern accoutrements grafted onto the old work. White plastic boxes with blinking LEDs sat against Bakelite and ceramic knobs, faded with time. Wires were spliced to wires, and the whole thing smelled musky. It smelled *old*.

The odour lingered in Joel's nostrils. The mess of wiring and cables hummed with current. His hands danced, wanting to plunge into the cabinet with some weird magnetism to touch the bare metal, feel the electrons surge through and pull his life into the ground with them.

Joel shook his head, scanning the panel with his eyes. Then he saw something that wasn't just cowboy, but criminal. It crackled.

He closed the cabinet and retreated back upstairs.

CHAPTER 9

Dallas Wentworth lived in a very nice house a world away from the concrete jungle of Chivron Tower. That autumn morning he woke in his king-size bed next to his wife Hickorie. She nuzzled back into the covers, a contented smile remaining on her face. Dallas smiled too. Every night in those Egyptian cotton sheets was like sleeping on a cloud of luxury, and he had the receipt to prove it.

'Mornin', he said, sitting at the breakfast bar in the expansive kitchen, as Hickorie walked in, dressed in a fluffy bathrobe, white as the virgin snow. More Egyptian cotton. 'Coffee?'

'I thought you wouldn't ask.'

Dallas poured his wife a steaming cup of coffee from the chrome-and-glass cafetiere. The first sip hit her lips like sugar, her nostrils widening to entrench the aroma. Her eyes fell open again, gazing through the curtain-glass walls onto the green, lush parcel of Surrey countryside that they could call theirs. Trees and hedgerows bordered the lawn, with a wooden hot tub at one end.

She glanced, mid-sip, at the clock on the wall. Putting down the cup, she looked to Dallas.

'No meetings this morning?'

He smiled. 'Later.'

The counter buzzed. Dallas glanced. *The work phone.* He picked it up. 'What?'

'Dad!' the voice called from the other end.

'Sweetness?' Dallas asked. His daughter Scarlett *never* called on the work phone. 'Wh-why are you calling me on the work phone?'

'Because you need to get here, pronto.'

'What's happened?' Dallas asked. He mouthed to Hickorie that it was a *work thing*, then moved into his home office. 'Are you alright?'

'Yes, but this bloody flat you stuck me in isn't!'

'Spoken to Mike?'

'He's here, but this is a big problem, Dad. You'd better get here. Before I really freak out.'

'Are you sure Mike can't-'

'*Do you want me to call mum?*' Scarlett said, knowing the answer before even finishing the question.

Dallas took a big breath. 'I'll be there as soon as, sweetness.'

The line clicked dead. He emerged from the office back into the expansive kitchen.

'Something the matter?' Hickorie asked. Dallas reached for his jacket and keys.

'Something has come up. I need to go into town.'

'When will you be back?'

'Soon, I promise, honey-suckle. Soon.'

On the motorway, the phone buzzed in Dallas's pocket. He eased it with one hand - it was an automatic gearbox, so he could and did do this with flagrant vulgarity - and held it against his ear with a shoulder.

'Sandy, always a pleasure.'

'Are you on your way up here?'

'By here would I be able to assume you mean the Chivron Tower?'

'Yeah.'

'On my way. Are you there?'

'I got here just before they did.'

'Who's they?'

'Aich 'n' Ess.'

'Has something happened?'

'It's under control. But it could be bad for us.'

'Any press.'

'No. Not that I know of.'

'Let's keep it that way. I'll see you in thirty.'

'You'd better.'

The Tower soon loomed in front of Wentworth's car, the engine idling to a stop where it had before on the previous visit, just in front of the entrance.

Without waiting, Wentworth climbed out. He saw people in suits and jackets milling around the lobby doors. His mouth puckered. *They looked official.* Quickly, one of the officials tapped toward the car.

'Sandy.'

'Dallas.'

'Tell me the problem.'

'Let's go inside.'

Councillor Grimms led the way through the doors, past the swish accoutrements of the entranceway and into the mechanical room. A trio of men were examining the wiring cupboard behind the lift. One of them turned.

'Boss.'

'Mike, what's happening?'

'One of the residents got a big bill. Three figures.'

'How is that out of the ordinary?'

'It's for one month.'

Wentworth cocked his head. 'I spend more than that on chardonnay some nights.'

'It's abnormal.'

'Which resident was it again?'

'Flat Forty-four. The Bartons.'

'Great,' Wentworth harumphed. 'So he gets a big bill, he doesn't want to pay it. Why, exactly, am I stood here, Mike?'

'He had a look in the wiring cupboard. He didn't like what he saw. And neither do I. Or Health and Safety. Can you smell that?'

Wentworth sniffed. His features wrinkled. 'Burning.'

'That,' Mike said, 'ain't half of it. Wait till you see why.'

Wentworth followed Mike back to the cramped space in the corner of the mechanical room. He glanced into the maw of the wiring cupboard.

'We ordinarily would've ripped it all out, as you know,' Mike began, 'but you didn't sign off on that.'

'If it ain't broke...'

'Well, it is, frankly. Everything in here is old grafted to new. Not how I would've done it, but new costs, as you well know.'

'Okay. Is there anything inherently dangerous about this? Apparently, I've got Aich 'n' Ess breathing down my neck.'

'They're just leaving,' Mike said. 'I talked to them.'

'Good.'

'But in answer to your question, Dal, yes there is.'

'Is it something *we* did?'

'Not initially, no.'

'So, what is it?'

'See here?' Mike indicated; his movement hesitant. The cabinet remained live. The hum of current buzzed around them. 'Someone's tapped into flat Forty-four's power. Actually it's the whole floor. The wiring's not made for that kind of load.'

'They must be mad,' Wentworth said. 'Our wiring or the original?'

Mike nodded. 'Both. Whatever they're doing, and they're drawing a lot of power, it's all been billed to Forty-four. They're probably getting billed for the whole floor. And whoever tapped in.'

Wentworth groaned. 'Great. Who should I talk to first?'

'We can disconnect this, but we have to shut the building

down. Every floor. Maybe you should give Mr. Barton the good news. He won't have to pay eight-hundred pounds for his power this month.'

'Mike, I think I'll do just that,' Wentworth said, shuffling out of the cramped, dark space and back into the airy, light-painted lobby. 'Shut it down and get it fixed.'

Mike nodded as Wentworth trooped outside. There he saw Councillor Grimms, where he'd been, still sucking on a cigarette.

'Good news, Dallas?'

'This was too close. Who exactly are you packing these flats full of? We had a deal. This, plus the shitload of emails I keep getting. Complaints. Anti-social behaviour. Maybe I should send them to you.'

Sandy Grimms held up his hands in a mocking gesture of surrender. 'Don't shoot me! Look, we've some trouble tenants to get rid of, they've caused us no end of trouble for us on other estates. Why not give 'em a taste of the high life in this exclusive new development.'

'Couldn't you just get rid? There's thirty boroughs you could've palmed them off to. Not my development.'

'But it's not strictly *yours*, is it? We did you a big favour, and you owe us, Dallas. Not in money, no, that would defeat the point of our arrangement, now, wouldn't it? We have a symbiotic relationship. You refurbish this eyesore that we'd wanted to tear down, we let you pretty it up, make a bit of dosh.'

'You don't need to remind me, Sandy...'

'And *in return*,' Sandy continued, 'you gave us, a poor, hard up town borough, thirty per-cent of the flats as social housing. Three times the usual. You kind soul. Discounted rates, seeing as your outlay was so much less. You get a third of the housing benefits too, we still charge the DWP the full whack. Creative accountancy. On top of all the other procedural favours. I shouldn't have to remind you of any of this, Dallas. Yet I am. Anyway, the point is, they're social tenants, and as such, we re-house them. It's almost like it was meant to be.'

Dallas took a big, deep breath. 'Point made, okay, Sandy. Still, I wish we'd talked about this more. I could've put a separate door in. You know, for the dregs.'

'I spoke to the Health and Safety people, as a concerned councillor, you do understand. It would be remiss of me in my position, you see. Head of the planning committee and all. Anyway,' he said, returning to Dallas, 'They seem satisfied by your man, Mike, which is good.'

'I'm pleased Mike did his job.'

'But you need to do yours. Aich 'n' Ess brings the foul stench of a dog with a bone to our door. And that could bring our arrangement under a spotlight it needn't find itself under. When did you last visit the Tower, Dallas?'

Dallas paused. 'Three months ago. Since Scarlett moved in.'

Grimms approached, flicking his now-finished cigarette away. 'And you say the Council treat it like a dumping ground?

'You know she goes to Uni not far from here.'

'How sweet. She gets a plum top-floor flat on daddy. Shame. This could've ended badly. I suggest, therefore, you pay a bit more attention to this development than you have been doing so as of late. For all our sakes.'

'I don't like that implication.'

'If the house of cards comes tumbling down, Dallas, I am going to climb up and bury you.'

'To save the poxy Council?'

'No. To save me.' the councillor finished with a lungful of used smoke into Dallas' face, which wrinkled.

Wentworth coughed. 'I'll go and give a resident some good news, he's saved a lot of money on his electricity this month.'

He walked back into the lobby as Sandy Grimms wordlessly watched from the corner of his eye.

There he saw a young lady emerge from the stairwell, throwing two rucksacks on the floor.

Their eyes met.

'Sweetn-'

'Just don't, Dad. Not after today,' Scarlett said back. 'I'm moving back to halls.'

'Now, please, isn't that a bit hasty.'

'There just isn't something right here.'

'A minor electrical problem, let's not jump to conclusions.'

Scarlett breathed. 'One more chance, Dad.' Dallas smiled. 'And you can carry those back up to twenty-three. Lift's busted.

Dallas' smile disintegrated.

'Yo, yo, man, we good for next week?' Royston bellowed into his phone. The music blaring from the stereo was obnoxious, the bass booming into the floors and walls.

Holding the phone tight to his ear with his shoulder, Royston hummed, milling into the master bedroom. There was no bed, however, but a multitude of foil tents. The material rustled as Royston pushed the structures open to reveal rows of plants under harsh halogen lights, surrounded by the reflective material of the tent-like structures.

'It's looking good, man, and I'll be able to keep this up for a long time I think!' Royston said, humming in assent to the reply. 'Alright fam, we'll touch base later.'

He hung up.

All the lights fizzled out simultaneously with a pop. The music stopped too, the silence filling the void where the dirty bass had pushed away.

'No, no!' Royston cried. He trudged to the power socket by the door. Four multi-gang plug strips were loosely hanging from the socket. The switch was on. Royston knelt and flicked the switch a couple of times. Nothing happened. The lights remained out. The flat silent.

He went back into the living room, wringing his hands behind his head in frustration. He paced around, in obscure and erratic patterns, looking all around, not sure what to do.

Then his focus returned. He looked, glancing the front door. He opened it after striding across and down the hallway. It clicked behind him. A piece of paper was taped loosely to the lift door. Royston tore it off as he approached.

LIFT OUT OF ORDER FOR EMERGENCY ELECTRICAL WORK

it said in crude, thick marker pen.

'Fuck!' Royston called, dropping the piece of paper and made for the stairs. He plodded down quickly, emerging into the Ground Floor lobby where he saw several people in high-viz vests. They took no heed of Royston, instead focussing on the mechanical room.

Royston followed around.

Excuse me, sir,' a man in a tieless suit asked. 'Can I help you?'

'You've cut all the power! You can't do this!' Royston replied, trying to hide the frustration - and panic - in his voice.

'Oh, did we not leave a sign? Emergency electrical work, we had to do it right now.'

'You didn't tell anyone!'

The man looked up for a moment. 'We did knock. Are you the man on the Seventh floor, loud music?'

Royston hesitated. 'Yeah, man. That's me.'

The man in the shirt smiled. 'We did try to knock but perhaps you didn't hear. We're sorry. But we must do this work now.'

'What work are you talking about?'

'Some crazy fool tapped the power cables to rack up a massive bill.' Then his eyes narrowed. 'What flat did you say you were from, again?'

'I didn't.'

The man in the shirt paused for a second. 'Okay, well, it should be back up in about an hour. Maybe two.'

'Man, you'd best make it one,' Royston said.

'We will do our best.'

Royston reached into his pocket. He pulled out a dirty wad of cash. He offered a rough handful of the notes to the man. 'Maybe this would, er, *incentivise* the lads.'

The man in the shirt looked at the cash. Then he looked up to Royston. 'Er, no, sorry. You see, we run a strictly legitimate operation here. I'm sure you appreciate that, but I can't make my men work with,' he gestured to the money, 'this. Sorry.'

With a scowl, Royston retreated.

Mike shook his head as the figure departed. He waved a hand in front of his face to dispel the pungent odour.

'Who was that?' one of the workmen asked.

'That,' Mike said, 'was probably our culprit.'

The workman didn't respond.

'Are we nearly done?' Mike then asked.

'Just tidying up now, Mike,' the man replied. 'Then do we get paid?'

Mike laughed. 'I'll have words with Mr. Wentworth. He'll pay you for this don't you worry. Easiest seven-fifty you lads have earned, I bet!'

The man laughed, as did his mate, who's chuckles were masked by the concrete wall.

'I think we're ready to switch on.'

'Let's see,' Mike said, sidling past. He examined the electrical closet. 'Not too fancy. It'll do.'

'You did say nothing special.'

Mike hummed. 'Let me do the honours...' he said, tailing off as he grasped the thick switch under his thumb and forefinger. He gave it a shove, and with a *thunk* it moved, the legend moving from black **off** to red **on**.

However, there was a sharp fizzle. A spark erupted underneath the yellowed plastic. The switch bounced back off. Mike backed off himself. 'That,' he hummed, 'shouldn't have happened.'

They were clearly in for an afternoon fighting with the electrics - just what everyone wanted.

Royston closed the door with a crack behind him. He pulled his phone from his tracksuit trousers as soon as the door had clicked. Fingers danced across the smudged glass.

'Surly, it's me. We've very quickly got a problem, blud.'

'Deal with it, Royston. We don't need this grief,' the voice on the phone blared. 'Sort it or ship out of there.'

CHAPTER 10

'Come in, come in! It's so great to see you!' Jules said. From the warm light of the landing outside, two figures in heavy winterwear came into the warmth.

'I don't like how cold that landing is. It's freezing,' the woman said.

'Should get that seen to, Julia,' the man added.

Jules paused. 'Yes, well, thank you, Dad. I'll add that to the list.'

'You do that,' Jules' dad said, letting his coat slide off into his daughter's waiting hand. With loud footsteps he clopped along the floor.

A door opened and the sound of fast, tiny footsteps filled the hallway.

'Grandad!' the twins called in unison.

Jules' dad smiled widely. 'Munchkins! It's so nice to see you! He knelt down, embracing the boy and girl. He released them after a moment, indicating to Jules' mum. 'Don't forget your nanny, too!'

'Nanny!' the children called in equal excitement.

'Well, I hope you don't think I'm kneeling down there!' Jules' mum laughed. 'Now, look, I brought you something.' She dug around in a plastic bag she carried. It was a tin of cupcakes.

'Thank you, Nanny!' Beth said.

'Can we have one now?' asked Ed.

'If you're good, maybe,' Jules' mum said. The children ran off into the living room.

'What,' Jules spat, 'are you doing that for?'

'Can I not treat my grandchildren?'

'We're about to have dinner. We've gone to a lot of effort, mum. We're trying to keep them on the straight and narrow.'

'Oh, don't worry about that dear, it's all a bit late isn't it.'

'Mum!'

A door clicked distantly.

'Hello Don, hello Theresa,' Joel said.

'Ah, Joel,' Don, Jules' dad responded, grasping his con-in-law's hand in a firm shake. 'Always a pleasure.'

'Isn't it just.'

Jules nudged him with her elbow. 'Joel!'

'It is, honestly! And Jules, don't leave your parents loitering in the hallway.' He turned to the in-laws. 'In, come in.'

They followed through to the living room and parked themselves on the couch in front of the not-immodestly-sized television that played, on mute, cartoons.

'Right,' Don huffed, grasping for the remote out of Ed's hand. 'Let granddad check on the horses. You like the horses, remember.'

Ed shook his head 'That's Beth who does.'

'Yeah, well, Granddad's got to watch 'em anyway. Move up, chuckles,' Don said falling back into the couch.

Joel joined his wife in the kitchen. Subtly, he pushed the door until it fell closed with nary a noise.

'Nearly showtime.'

'I know.'

'You know he's bound to bring it-'

'Not now, Joel. Not now. Now just help me with the dinner and we can get through this.'

Joel nodded and picked up two plates of steaming food. Jules picked up two smaller plates and motioned. 'You first.'

'Thanks,' Joel said, going through. He placed the two plates in front of Don and Theresa. Jules followed, placing the plates that she carried in front of the twins opposite. 'Oh,' she said.

'I hope you don't mind,' Don said, thrusting the bottle of wine that had appeared toward her. 'Get us a glass, then.'

Jules turned, hiding her sharp, deep breath as she walked into the kitchen.

'He hasn't has he?' Joel asked.

'He has.'

Joel swallowed. Jules disappeared with a wine glass from the cupboard. She then returned to the kitchen. Wordlessly, he and Jules took their own food and sat at opposite ends of the table.

'You know,' Don began, 'there was a lot of mess down by the doorway when we came in. Not what we expected.'

'Okay,' Jules retorted. 'I'll mention that.'

'Well, the point is,' Don continued, glugging on the glass of wine. 'More of that, please, keep it coming,' he said, shaking a hand. He coughed. Returning to the original point: 'I don't see much neighbourhood pride here. And that,' he took a deep breath. 'That saddens me.'

'Don,' Theresa said. 'Let's not get all up-in-arms over something small like that.'

'Small?!' Don said, this time louder. 'Woman, do you never listen to a word I say to you? We've - well, I say *we*, I earned it all, you're just there to make it look nice-'

'Dad!' Jules barked.

Theresa's lips tensed and pursed. 'I'm sorry dear, it's been a bad week, he's never usually like-' she began.

'Don't tell me what I'm like!' Don said.

'Dad,' Beth called. 'I'm not hungry all of a sudden.'

'You and your brother, go play in your room,' Joel urged. 'I'll bring your food in a minute-'

The children fled the table, needing no further encouragement.

'Dad, now, stop!' Jules barked. 'You've scared the kids now.'

79

'They're not youngsters, Julia. When, oh when,' Don ranted, taking a deep breath, 'will you realise this and just do what's to be done? I'm the only one here speaking up, I'm looking after an investment. It's a shame I'm the only one who seems concerned about it! I knew this was a mistake-'

'What, coming to dinner?'

Don gave Joel a severe look.

Joel coughed. 'Well, we've done the flat up very nicely wouldn't you agree?'

Don looked around, rolling his eyes. 'I suppose. But if it were me I'd have-'

'But it's *not* you, is it Dad?' Jules said. 'I wish I'd never asked, now.'

'Look, wasn't it your mother's idea to come over tonight? I knew I wasn't quite feeling it but here we are.'

'Yes, here we are. Thank you, Dad for totally being like you always have been.'

'What do you mean? Julia?'

She took a big breath. 'I wish I'd never asked you for that eighty-grand, alright. But we fell in love with this place and I thought it would be nice of you, for the first real time in your life, to do something for your family.'

'Jules, take it easy,' Joel said. He grasped at her clutching hand, feeling it tremble.

'Listen,' Don blustered. 'I did what- what?' His face descended, vampire-like into a peak. 'You always were ungrateful. You don't even use the name we gave you. *Jules*. And the home you keep is surrounded by a bunch of dole-claiming vagabonds.'

'Shut up, Dad, alright, just please, just shut up for one moment!'

The dining area fell silent for a moment.

'Well, I think I'll just relieve myself,' Don said, scraping his chair against the laminate floor as he shot to his feet.

'Bloody thing,' Don cursed, lifting the toilet seat. With a

wheeze, he desecrated the porcelain. Then, getting up with a bigger wheeze, he reached for the handle. It depressed, too easily. The fixture gurgled.

'Huh.'

Don stepped toward the basin sink. He grabbed the hot tap handle. It spun. More gurgles, followed by vicious spits of grey and brown water, splashing right onto the white china. He flinched. New plumbing shouldn't do that.

The pipe sounded like it was coughing a deep, throaty gurgle. Dirty water spackled onto the porcelain. Deep in the pipes, there was a gruff rumble. More water spat from the taps, leaving smears of brown and grey on the white sink.

'What the hell is happening in here?!' he said.

Jules swept toward the bathroom. 'Look, Dad, I really don't want to have to deal with this on top of everything else tonight...'

'No, Jules,' Don said. 'Look at this!'

She rushed over to the sink. 'What the hell did you do?'

'It wasn't me!' Don responded.

'Joel!' Footsteps followed the cry.

'Christ, what's-'

'Listen! I didn't touch those damn taps. They started doing it all by themselves. Listen!'

The three of them glanced to the sink. Not a sound came from the fixture.

'Dad...' Jules sighed, walking to the sink past Don. She turned the cold tap and then the hot tap. A steady, serene stream of crystal-clear water flowed for a few moments before she shut them off.

'I'm telling you, Julia, I did not flood this bathroom myself. That's the god's honest!'

She took a big breath. 'Dad, I think you need some real help.'

'Are you mad, woman?!'

'You know what happens when you have a drink. I'll call you a cab.'

'I'm not sozzled, Julia, you just aren't-'

'Please, Dad, don't make this harder. I'll clear this up in a bit,' she said to Joel. With a disappointed look, she glanced at Don before moving away.

He turned himself, back to the tap.

It growled, just enough for him to hear, like it was *laughing*, but by that time the argument was lost.

CHAPTER 11

In flat Fifteen, Krystal negotiated around a pile of boxes – identical – televisions and games consoles - and into an equally chaotic kitchen.

'Teej,' she hollered, to no answer. She knew where he was anyway. Balancing around the various obstacles formed of stalactites of cutter, she wobbled. It was enough to send one of the piles crashing to the floor. 'Fuck,' she exclaimed, the words slipping out of her mouth subconsciously, without her even knowing. She ditched the ball of creased laundry on the sofa.

What had also fallen to the floor were letters that she should have kept in better order than she did already. The pile was quite substantive - a dozen and a half, all dated recently, all addressed to flat Fifteen, but regarding a variety of people who didn't live there.

The letterhead however, like the address, was identical: DWP.

The names, though, were fictitious.

Krystal was not impoverished though, as the pile of letters symbolised her sustenance.

She went to find TJ. Even at this hour, late afternoon, it was time to get busy.

The bedroom was, like the rest of the flat, a litany of rubbish, with bags left with their contents vomited out of them. What TJ called a bed - a loose assemblage of tussled bedding atop a worn, manky mattress.

'Get up. We've got the inspector coming.' TJ murmured, but it wasn't intelligible. 'I said up!'

'Piss off, woman,' TJ yawned. He scratched himself indiscreetly, then threw the threadbare duvet aside, leaving it in the heap he threw it in. 'You got my money?'

'Money?' Krystal retorted. 'Man, that's all you think about, isn't it TJ?'

He yawned again, and promptly belched. 'Got it or no?'

She rolled her eyes and stuck a hand down the back pocket of her joggers. A dirty great wad of notes came out, bundled up. She allocated roughly half of it by eye and thrust it into his hand. He regarded it, and then held out his hand again.

'You wanna count it?'

'Do I have to?' TJ teetered. He looked around, through the sea of mess. He picked up one of the half-empty cans of cheap lager. He drank a loose mouthful, the flat liquid running down his face. He belched again.

'No, you know I do it right,' she said. He put on a pair of expensive trainers. Then he motioned past her, shouldering her out of the way of the door. She turned. 'Where are you going?'

'Out,' he said without looking.

'No,' she said. 'You can't.'

He stopped. She gulped. Then he turned, his face blackened and twisted.

'What did you say, *bitch*?'

Krystal shivered. 'Well, we have the inspector coming, and, well, look, we need to-'

'We?!' he said. Then he stepped over to her. He jabbed in her chest, right in the middle on the breastplate. 'You need to. I'm. Going. Out.'

'Oh, Teej,' she started, 'please, I, I...'

'You what? Need me? Fuck off, Krystal. You're pathetic.'

'Teej!' she shouted.

'*I said I was going out!*' He yelled back. 'Oh, look,' he continued,

84

'you going to cry?'

'N-no,' she said. She sniffed. He stepped forward.

'When, oh *when*, Krystal, will you realise who I am? I ain't cleaning up your shit. You're a woman, that's what you do.'

'What are you going to do?' she trembled. 'Have my money, Teej, please, I can't-'

He shook his head. 'You wake me up with this shit?! I need to wash your mouth out. Stop you saying these, these...' he gesticulated, 'these really dumb things.'

Then, before she could react, he lunged and grabbed her by the scruff of the neck, like a normal person might grab a dog in its infancy to teach it some manners. Dragging her behind him, he pushed past one of the doors of the flat that wasn't hanging off. The bathroom beckoned. He pulled on the light-cord and the spotlights illuminated the scene.

She protested. The toilet seat was flung up with a thud of plastic against china.

'Kneel,' he said. She hesitated. 'Kneel!'

He made her kneel with a push of his own kneecap into the back of her legs. Then, now prone, TJ thrust her face toward the toilet bowl. The water gurgled and rippled, going dark with shadow.

'This is about me, you know. You think we're a partnership. Like some normal bullshit married couple. But we're not. You know what you are?'

She shook her head.

TJ nodded to the bowl. 'You're what ends up in there.'

Before she could answer he thrust her face directly into the water with one hand, and, kneeling on her back just to hold her down, reached for the handle. A cascade of water descended from the rim of the bowl and drenched Krystal, the water becoming muddied with makeup that washed off her face.

After a few moments, the cascade of water went away. Krystal took a deep, soulful lungful of breath.

'You learned, yet?' TJ bellowed.

'Stop, stop,' she moaned. 'Look, why can't we-' she said, her words cut off.

'What, bitch?' TJ asked. Krystal didn't move. Instead, she just looked, to the side, toward the bath. A soft grinding sound came from the tub. TJ pivoted. 'The actual *fuck?*'

From the tub, the loose shower head rose like a serpent on the end of its hose. Behind it, a booming, banging sound from deep within the wall.

The showerhead clicked. From the pipe behind it came a rumble. TJ dropped Krystal with a soft thud. He stepped toward the bathtub. The showerhead, suspended in the air, backed off, just a little. Then it leant back and, with an even-throatier clank, spat a glug of hissing water into TJ's face.

'Ah, *fuck!*' TJ screamed, clutching at his face. The showerhead then danced around, spitting more glugs of steaming water into his face. Staggering, TJ lunged. The showerhead dodged, the spits of water now becoming a constant gushing torrent. The bathroom filled with the sound of the running water hitting the white tub and TJ's screaming. 'Get it off, get it off!'

Eventually he turned, his front sodden and his face red from scalding. He moved his fingers delicately, finally opening his eyes. He met Krystal's gaze. She fled, backing into the door, which slammed closed. 'You bitch! You did this!' Lunging forward, he missed. 'I know you did this, somehow, you *fucking evil bitch.* Argh!' TJ fell, slipping on the water on the floor. The hose of the showerhead wrapped around his legs. It tugged him back toward the bath. The hose released from TJ's legs just a bit, allowing the showerhead itself to rise up above him. It lunged back, then sprayed another torrent of the steaming water right into his face.

His scream became a gargle, then it became a raucous cough for breath. He began to turn over, to be face-down on the sodden floor, the drenched bathmat crumpling under his flailing. Now prone, he looked up, seeing Krystal hunched against the door.

'Fuck you, Krystal,' he hissed. 'I'm gonna fucking-' he started, but didn't finish. The showerhead had wrapped around his neck. It tightened. He grasped at the hose with his scalded fingers, the red flesh clutching at the silvery metal. But they slipped, and he retched, trying to breathe through the mist and torrent of steaming water blasting on his face again. He tried to pull himself up using the towel-rail as a scaffold, but he simply slipped, one last time, falling onto the edge of a bath with a sick, wet *thwack*.

The showerhead dropped instantly back into the tub, upside down, to form a fountain of pencil-thin streams.

And there was no more noise, just the running water.

A few moments passed, then Krystal moved. TJ's form didn't; it was slumped over the bath, his legs dangling limp.

Getting to her feet, she leant over the bath to turn the water of. 'Oh my god,' she inhaled. The bottom of the bath was smeared red. After a couple of false starts, she reached in, leaning over. The showerhead sprayed her harmlessly with warm water which splashed down her front. She turned the valve with a squeak, and the water stopped.

TJ didn't move.

Turning, she pitter-pattered through the water on the floor and ran out of the flat.

But there was no escape. She glanced down through the stairwell window. A car she hadn't wanted to see was arriving in the car park downstairs. She turned, back into her flat, and put a hand around the bathroom door. She felt for the light pull and clicked it, then, without looking inside, closed the bathroom door with a shiver.

CHAPTER 12

Under the blanket of sleep, Beth and Ed snoozed, breathing lightly. Cool wintry air buffeted the Tower, pushing into the crevices. The bedroom window rattled, just slightly.

The ceiling above the children tremored, just once. Then it buzzed again.

The children turned, their subconscious still directing their slumber.

But their ears prickled.

The ceiling boomed again, in a series of staccato thuds that resonated down into the open air of the children's' bedroom.

It became rhythmic, laced with musical interludes.

'Ed,' Beth whispered. 'Ed, wake up!'

'Go away,' he spat, his eyes still closed. Then he opened them. 'What?'

The ceiling tingled. Ed looked up, then back to the glistening orbs that were his sister's eyes.

'Not again,' he bemoaned, resigning himself to getting up.

'Let's go,' she said, taking the lead this time. Her hand reached for the handle. It turned with slick creak.

She went outside first, followed by her brother in nervous steps.

This time it was totally different.

She stopped dead, just on the threshold of the doorway to the rest of the flat.

'What?' Ed urged.

She shushed and pointed next door.

'Oh,' her brother said, looking at their parents' door.

It was open, revealing a maw of darkness with a glinting panel of moonlight cast from the window onto the bed.

It was empty. Unmade and the sheets crumpled, but *empty*.

Footsteps followed this revelation.

Ed turned, shoving his sister back into the bedroom. The door began to sweep closed behind them, pushed by small limbs. The children squealed, ever so quietly, but perceptibly, and they hurried into their room. There the music continued, thudding through the ceiling.

Falling into bed, the children gasped.

Behind them, the door opened. The music got louder, soaking in through the opening.

Peeking from under their duvets, the children saw a figure in the doorway, blotted out by the darkness. It stepped forward, out of the shadows, which made the children emit another involuntary peep.

'You hear it too?' the figured murmured.

'Dad!' Beth said. She exhaled. Ed did the same, hopping out of his bed.

'It's that music,' the boy said. 'I don't know what it is.'

'Let's find out,' Joel said. He nodded over his shoulder.

'Can we come?' Beth asked.

'We're the only ones who can hear it,' Joel said. 'It's scary up there.'

'We have to,' Ed added. 'It's not going away. Can Mum hear it?'

'Don't worry about her,' Joel said, turning. 'Get dressed. It's not going away, is it? It's just us.'

Both children shook their heads, before quickly throwing their old clothes atop their pyjamas. Then, with their dad leading in his own dressing-gown, they headed out and to the lift.

The lift juddered to a stop at the Twenty-Third Floor.

'Huh', Joel noted. He'd not been up here in a long time.

Outside of the lift, the music thudded in space between flats with definition. It called down through the concrete ceiling.

This was beyond a figment of their imagination. This music was so loud and clear it had to be real.

But the landing was totally dark. Joel reached into his pocket and produced his phone. He swiped, activating the flashlight feature.

What he saw took his breath from his lungs.

The walls were caked in detritus, dirt and cobwebs that hung in a very, very subtle breeze. These cobwebs heaved with the beat of the music from above. The floor was thick with a layer of brown dust. Joel's foot left boot prints like those left on the moon's rocky surface.

'What's happened up here?' he asked to no-one. The children stayed quiet.

'I want to go back,' Beth said, turning back to the lift. She lifted a finger to press the button, but yelped.

'What?!' Joel said, turning. He approached the lift. It was buzzing with electricity. 'Don't touch it again. Looks like we're here now.'

They turned around, looping back around the lift. The front doors to the empty flats were coated in the cobwebs and grime. It was as if no-one had been up here to clean in forty years. But this was at odds with the modern paint and panelling.

Time had crept back in, the true age and core of Chivron Tower bursting through its new façade.

'Dad,' Ed murmured, 'look. Over here.'

Joel followed his son around the corner. 'Sh-' He began, catching himself. 'Sugar.'

Usually, the children would giggle at this, but not now. A broken wall beckoned, the jagged rubble of the blocks facing out into the corridor. *Something had broken out. Something not contained by walls...*

Behind the rough break in the new blockwork, the darkness beyond. This darkness was threaded by beads of a curious and wispy turquoise energy. And the steady, beating thrum of the music that came, as the grime all around did, from a distant past.

The three of them stood on the precipice, where the smashed blockwork met the new lino on the floor.

'Come up, then,' a voice called. The three of them stood bolt upright, shocked by the voice. 'Don't be afraid.' Joel took the first step. The voice boomed again. 'All of you.'

The children looked at each other. Then they looked to their dad.

'Guess we'd better go, kids,' he said, turning to the opening. 'It's going to get worse before it gets better.' Then, with a last deep breath of stale air, he stepped over the broken blocks and went up the stairs.

The penthouse was brightly illuminated, but empty. The rot that had been there before seemed frozen, but the jukebox against the swollen wood panelling glittered with neon light.

'Take a seat,' the voice called. Joel looked to the collapsing couch in front of the television. 'Yes, there,' the voice said again. 'Go on, go on!' it urged.

Joel held the children's hands and pulled them toward the settee. It was in a slight depression in the living space, down some very shallow steps and past a panelled half-wall. This looked over a vista of the modern, vibrant city beyond. This vibrant world had enveloped the time the Tower had come from.

'What do you want?' Joel said above the music. It stopped abruptly with a click. 'That's better.'

'I think,' the voice said, 'it's time you saw my real form.'

The lights clicked out. Joel and the twins took a single breath. Then the lights fizzed back into life. Behind them, a shuffling.

'Who are you?' Beth called.

A figure emerged, out of nowhere, almost, into the light of the living area. 'I'm the Architect,' the figure replied. It sat down opposite the Bartons. The cracked and worn leather of the settee creaked. The three seated occupants withdrew. 'I think it's about time we met and talked. It's been so long, and things... well, they're not going well, wouldn't you agree?' The figure flourished a bony hand. 'Excuse my manners. Would you like a drink? I left you some on the table, look,' the Architect gestured. The children cast a glimpse to the coffee table just in front of them. Three cloudy glasses of bright-yellow liquid sat on frayed coasters. The children froze. Joel, however, looked back to the Architect.

'Who are you?'

'I already said, didn't you hear? I am the Architect. Herve Chivron, master builder and designer of this architectural wonder piece. We have a symbiotic relationship, the Tower and I.'

Joel blinked, not responding. 'You're not. Wentworth is the architect. Or the owner. Or whatever it is he is.'

The Architect snapped. 'He is not! He is a pretender. We have spoken, though, him and I.'

'And what did you say to him?'

The Architect took a seat on the opposite sofa. 'I told him I thought he had ruined my beautiful building. I told him that it all had to go back to how it was. Or there would be consequences. He didn't listen, he didn't stop. Hence I engineered this meeting. I'm very selective of who I make my presence known to.'

Joel laughed. 'I saw the brochure when I bought the flat. No-one had touched this place for years. They were going to pull it-'

'They were not! They couldn't do such a thing! I wouldn't let them, you see. The Tower can't be destroyed,' the Architect said. In a low rumble, he qualified: 'not by mortal hands, anyway. The basement. Yes,' the Architect trailed off, breaking focus with Joel. But the Architect's gaze snapped back. 'Time's running out...'

'Uh-huh.'

'Dad,' Beth cooed, huddling closer to her father. 'Who is this guy?'

Joel looked back to the Architect, watching his grey, pallid features wrinkle and wheeze, without an answer to his daughter. 'You're scaring my children.'

The Architect turned his head slightly. 'Am I scaring you, little girl? Shame.' Then he turned back to Joel. 'I told that Wentworth man he had to restore the Tower. I thought I could control things, it worked out well with you, yes... but then the others came. You know the sort,' the Architect continued quickly. 'I warned him. To how it was. Empty, but pristine. He had to take out all the rubbish.'

'We put ours in the chute-'

'No, not the *rubbish*. The *people*! I'm sure you've seen. You're outnumbered, you all are!'

'You really think you're going to get us to leave?'

'It's too late to discriminate between the good and the bad. There's a critical mass, you see.'

'Of what?'

'I-' the Architect wheezed but then grasped his body in apparent agony. 'You don't understand. The forces that allow the Tower to keep me alive they're-' the Architect howled. 'I knew it was too soon,' the Architect said, facing the wall. He got up, and slammed both hands as balled fists against the wall. He'd forgotten all about the Bartons. 'Why are you *doing this to me*?'

Joel and the two children scattered to their feet, making quickly for the way out.

'Consider this your warning, too, resident,' the Architect said, turning his arched figure to them. 'I didn't think I would warn you, but I am feeling... charitable, yes.'

'This is sick,' Joel said. 'Come on, kids.'

'But Dad-' Ed started.

'No, Ed,' Joel said. 'Look, I don't really understand what's happening. Maybe I don't want to. But we're living here, and we won't live in fear.' He pushed them toward the stairwell. He turned before descending. 'I don't understand what your problem is, or even who the hell you are. What you are. But you don't scare me, and you don't scare my family.'

'I'll win, you do understand this? Things,' the Architect took a long crack of his dry neck bones, 'things will get worse. For everyone. For you. Don't be a fool. Don't become collateral.'

Joel scoffed. 'Is it really so bad having actual people living in a nice building?'

'It's not as I designed it to be. And it is not filled with the people it was designed to house. These things are a confluence, and it will end in folly.'

'You designed a shithole. Face the facts, it was getting worse. I've made a home here, with my family. Lots of people have. Lots of nice people.'

'Are you sure? Nothing goes in in my Tower without me knowing. I've seen. I know. *It knows.*'

Joel paused. 'The overwhelming majority are nice people here. We go to work, pay our service charge and we keep the building looking nice.'

'The Tower is bound in a corset of polyvinyl cladding,' the Architect retorted. 'That hides the inner beauty, the highlights of the-'

'It's not the Seventies. Get with the times. Kids,' Joel said to Beth and Ed, 'let's go back to bed.' He turned to the Architect once more. 'Leave my family be. Stay in your rotten penthouse for all I care. But I don't want to see or hear from you ever again. You got me?'

'The cleaners will come to take out the rubbish-'

'No, they won't. Maybe the rubbish would be easier to get rid of if you hadn't designed the chutes so badly.'

The Architect bellowed a hearty laugh. 'The rubbish – one way or the other – will be cleaned and recycled. That's all I'll say on the matter.'

Joel looked at him, unsure of a response. Then he tore his head away, remembering. He urged the children down the stairs, away from the raucous, haunting laughter.

Downstairs, the children ran back into flat Forty-four, letting the door slam. They went straight to their room and buried their heads in the duvets and blankets.

Jules emerged from the bedroom clutching her pyjamas closed. She saw Joel, standing, breathing heavily in the hallway, panting in the darkness.

CHAPTER 13

Once again, a mobile phone buzzing on a bedside table disrupted a serene morning in the Surrey foothills.

Bzzt. Bzzt. Bzzt.

Wentworth moaned, still groggy. The snow-white sheets crinkled. Rubbing his eyes, he reached for the phone, but missing.. Finally, his wandering hand found the phone and tugged, pulling it from the charging mat it lay on. The phone found his cheek.

'What?'

Mike barked. 'Get to Chivron, now.'

'What?'

'Barton is demanding to see you. And if you don't show up, expect big trouble. His words, not mine. Though you didn't speak to him, he sounded completely-'

'That's enough! Christ, alright. I'll get on the road.' Wentworth yawned. He pulled himself out of bed and sat the phone back on its mat. He tapped the screen. 'What's actually happened now?'

'There was an incident on the Twenty-third Floor,' the voice on the other end of the phone said.

'I thought we'd sorted out that problem before?'

'Clearly you didn't, or something's happened.'

'Let me get dressed and I'll get there and put it right once and for all.'

'Need a building team there?'

'No,' Wentworth said. 'I'll call and let you know.'

The phone went dead, and Wentworth let it fall onto the soft duvet. He sighed and busied himself getting dressed, glancing back to the bed. His wife yawned, opening her eyes.

The phone buzzed again a moment later. Wentworth answered it.

'Sweetness-'

'Have you spoken to Mike?' Scarlett said. 'He said he was ringing you. All bloody night, something upstairs kept me up. Someone and their shitty kids up and down those bloody-'

'Alright, I'm on my way,' Wentworth said. He hung up again.

'Did the phone go off?'

'It did,' Wentworth said quickly.

'It's so early, Dal,' she said. 'Why are you getting dressed?'

'I have to go. It's a work thing.'

She shook her head. 'You'll work yourself to death, you know.'

'Probably,' he said, not really listening. He pulled on some smart jeans and a crinkled shirt. It wouldn't matter. Finally, he put on his jacket and a scarf. The wind had been fierce that previous evening. 'I'll be back soon, alright?'

'Gimme a kiss,' she said, puckering her lips and pushing her face forward.

Instead, the door just clicked.

Hickorie Wentworth opened her eyes, surprised, and fell back into bed.

The car revved away on the gravel, chips flying in its wake. Soon, Dallas found himself zipping up the motorway. At this time of day it was deserted. Wentworth's foot nudged the accelerator, the needle on the speedo rising. Sixty. Seventy. Eighty. Dallas dodged what few cars there were, their slow-moving forms like icebergs on a sea of grey asphalt.

The needle soon touched ninety without even thinking.

Dallas fumbled with his phone, trying to place it into the cradle on the central console. His attention - and eyes - wandered.

He leant to his left, the phone falling from his grasp. It hit the floor of the footwell.

'Fuck,' he cursed, and reached down, initially trying to keep an eye on the road. But the footwell was deep, and he glanced down. For three seconds his left hand grasped, finally pulling the phone up and dumping it in the cupholder below the central console.

Then his eyes looked back to the road. What he saw made him gasp.

'Shit, no!' Dallas called, pulling the wheel back, overcompensating for the drift that pushed the car toward the big, filthy truck in the adjacent lane. The truck honked, anticipating an impact. But Dallas grasped the wheel once more and overcorrected the other way, the tyres screeching. The long front of the car lurched, snaking left and right - this time it would surely hit one of the cars in front - metal icebergs in the ocean of road ahead.

Roaring, Dallas' car weaved past a junction. From a layby emerged the sleek, shadowed silhouette of a motorway patrol car. They'd seen enough.

Blue-and-red flashes flickered into Dallas' rear-view mirror, followed by fitful bursts of a siren. It was enough to grab his attention.

'Great,' he cursed. His foot hesitated over the accelerator, hovering in automotive stasis. He glanced at the car behind him, it got closer. His eyes narrowed, flickering down to the instrument panel. 'Whatever,' he exhaled. The car slowed, eventually rolling to a stop on the hard shoulder.

The engine idled. In the wing mirror, Dallas saw the policeman emerge from the car, the yellow hi-viz a contrast against the grey sky. Another remained seated inside the traffic car, staring into his lap. *Writing the ticket already, the bastard.*

The policeman approached and tapped the window with a knuckle. Dallas wound the window down, letting the hissing noise of the motorway and the ambience of the autumn morning enter the car's insulated cabin.

'Can I help, officer?' Dallas mouthed.

The policeman shook his head. 'You know what you were doing?'

Dallas nodded. 'I think so. Look, I'll take the ticket, I'm sorry, but I don't have time for this. No offence.'

'No-one ever does. Step out of the car, sir, and take a seat in my vehicle.'

Dallas gripped the steering wheel. His knuckled whitened. 'Like I said, please, just ticket me and let me go, please.'

'Why,' the officer asked. 'Got somewhere you need to be?'

'Yes!' Dallas shouted. The officer moved back. 'Sorry, I didn't mean to shout, look, yes, I have to... important meeting with a client. They've...'

'Slow down,' the officer hushed. Dallas heard the door latch click. The drivers' door swung open into the coldness outside, pulling the heat with it. 'Sit in my vehicle, I'll take your details.'

'Doesn't that fancy computer of yours have 'em already?' Dallas shivered, but the officer didn't move.

The officer reached in, turned the engine off, and pocketed the key. 'Now.'

Dallas hissed through his teeth, released his seatbelt and climbed out, stepping onto the gritty tarmac.

The walk to the patrol car was only a few yards but the environment was hostile. Spray from the occasional passing vehicle, mixed with the grittiness of a British autumn day. The officer opened the back door. Dallas' legs folded and he took a seat. A few moments passed, and the officer took his seat in the front once again.

'Right,' the officer began, fingering through a notebook. 'I'm police constable Kenny. This is my colleague, constable Shawn. I clocked you at one-hundred-and-seven miles per hour when I stopped you. And I saw you weaving all over the road, pretty erratically. You know you nearly went into that big truck?'

'Yes,' Dallas responded. 'I'm sorry, alright. Look,' he began, fishing into his pockets. He pulled out his wallet, and from within that, a pink licence photocard. 'There's my details.'

'Dallas Wentworth,' PC Kenny read. 'Quite a name.'

'It is what it is.'

'What happened with that truck then?'

'I dropped my phone. That's all.'

Sssshhhttt. Kenny sucked through his teeth. 'Driving without due care...'

'Look,' Dallas said. 'I'm in a hurry. Wouldn't anyone else be if you saw them driving like that?' He glanced at his watch. 'Shit, Christ, I'm meant to be there by now. Look, please, officer, just give me the bloody ticket.'

'Easy now,' Kenny said. 'We all have places to be. But we all have to do so in a careful and considerate manner, it's not just you on the road.'

'It more or less is, though!'

'And at-'

'Look,' Dallas pouted. 'I really, *really* don't need this, alright. It's six-thirty on a Sunday-'

'You listen pal!' officer Kenny barked. 'You are going to hear what I have to say and the more you whinge, the slower this is going to take.'

Dallas shook his head in disbelief, then craned it back against the headrest. 'Fine, say what you have to say.'

'Thank you,' the officer said. He turned, facing forwards again, palming through his notebook. 'Now, I'll issue you a...'

The officer was drowned out by a blaring horn.

'Look out!' Dallas yelled, pointing forward.

On the opposite side of the carriageway, an articulated lorry roared through under a concrete bridge. The lorry wobbled. Just to the side, a small car overcompensated, careering in front of

101

the artic. The cab toppled under the force of the brakes, but a collision was unstoppable.

Emerging from under the bridge, the artic clipped the faded Ford Ka in front of it. The Ka, pushed sideways on by the truck, veered off. The truck veered in the opposite direction - across the carriageway and through the crash-barriers that crumpled into twisted steel ribbons.

Soaring over the central reservation, the artic jack-knifed with a jump. The trailer barrel-rolled across the carriageway. Cars ducked like furtive ants in a siren of horns and screeching rubber.

But the police car on the hard shoulder remained stationary. The wreck of the lorry catapulted across the tarmac, right for the police car.

In the back seat, Dallas Wentworth shielded his face with his arms.

Constable Shawn in the driving seat looked up, surprised. His mouth fell open, but no words came out. The crashing din from outside - pockmarked by skidding of tyres and honking of horns - closed in and enveloped the police car. The impact threw the car back. The car rolled down the ditch at the side of the tarmac. It buffeted the occupants through the roll, and glass shattered with each thud of collision.

Dallas' head hit the pillar and he sighed as his vision blacked out, the sound continuing for a few moments before he fell limp.

Eventually though, the light returned, and Dallas tried to move.

He couldn't, not painlessly anyway.

The police car was now inverted, the windows completely smashed. Out of the twisted window frame, nearby, the smoking wreck of the artic.

No sounds from the front though. Dallas fidgeted, and loosened himself from the inverted position he found himself in. He felt aches but no breaks.

Wriggling free of the wrecked police car, Dallas dodged around the wreck of the tractor. Beyond it, miraculously, his car sat there, covered in light debris but otherwise undamaged. Debris surrounded it but the paint was unblemished by the surrounding destruction.

Something in Dallas elicited a smile. He looked into the destroyed police cruiser. Both officers in front were stationary, their faces mashed with blood. Dallas looked around. Neither officers seemed to move. His hand darted in and fumbled. With a tinkle, the keys followed his hand out of Officer Kenny's pocket. With a hop and a wince of pain, and clutching his bruised leg, Dallas fell into his car.

A trembling hand put key into the lock and the engine purred to life. A glance in the mirror revealed the mayhem that had taken over the motorway. With a sucking of air through his teeth, Dallas accelerated away from his lucky escape, hardly able to contain a twisted, humourless laugh.

What absolute luck, he thought, long may it continue.

CHAPTER 14

Chivron Tower loomed ahead as Dallas turned through the residential streets. Through the windscreen he saw its angular form against the featureless grey sky, like a monolith.

He breathed in, letting the car glide to a stop where it had done the previous two times he had been compelled to visit.

The engine idled, then stopped completely. The only sound in the car Dallas' heavy breathing.

Even that stopped. Dallas opened the door, letting the ambient sound of the air outside surround him. He got out and stepped toward the entrance, not even locking the door.

The key was still in the ignition, dangling away next to the dollar-sign-shaped keyring that symbolised its owner.

The lobby was quiet and cold. Dallas hunched his coat closer to him. On autopilot, he approached the lift, only pulling a hand out of his pocket to jab at the call button.

He pressed it. Nothing. Glancing above the steel door, the floor indicator remained on Twenty-three. *Nobody lives up there*, Dallas thought. *So why is the elevator up there-* He shook his head. He didn't want to think about that. He jabbed the button again. Nothing. Not a rumble of mechanism, a trill of electricity, nothing.

Footsteps approached the stairwell door from above. The door flung open. Dallas glanced.

'Sweetness...'

'Don't,' Scarlett said, her voice quivering. She pushed the suitcase through the door. 'I'm out of here.'

'Scarlett, there was traffic. Where's Mike?'

'Ask him yourself,' she said, walking past toward the outside. 'I'm not spending one minute more here.'

'Want me to take you home?' Dallas protested.

'No,' Scarlett said, holding the door. 'George is – oh, look,' she said as a car entered the estate. 'I'll call mum and speak to her.'

'Honey...'

'Later, Dad, alright,' she said, letting the door close behind her.

Dallas turned back to the lift. The floor indicator hadn't changed. He pushed the button again, then thudded his palm against the lift door.

It opened, Dallas falling back. The lift wasn't there; instead a dark portal to nothingness.

'Fine,' he spat, turning on his heels for the stairway door. He pushed through with his shoulder, then gazed up and began the climb.

Eventually, reaching the Twelfth Floor, Dallas hesitated on the landing inside the stairwell. He faced a junction - the stairs continuing up, or the door to the Landing, where Flat Forty-four waited. He took long, thoughtful glances between the two. He was halfway to one place, but all the way to perhaps an easier resolution. Then he could go home.

This had to be the last time.

'No,' he said under his breath, to the emptiness itself. He turned to continue up the stairs, scowling at the door as he passed. 'I'll give you good news.'

The climb continued. Dallas felt, as the stairs disappeared underfoot, the coldness at the top of the building. It was creeping down the stairs, getting under his coat, pickling on his raw, bare skin.

The Sixteenth floor.

The Twentieth floor.

The Twenty-second floor. Now his breath, in and out in hard, shallow labours, formed clouds in front of his face.

He stopped on the break in the stairs, just before the door to the landing.

'Come on, Mr. Wentworth,' a voice called from the last stairwell past the Twenty-second floor. The Architect. Dallas glanced toward the last stairwell. He saw it was encased in brown detritus: a mix of hardened cobwebs fused into a glassy-like material. It clung to the walls and dirt suspended in a gloop. 'We need to talk.'

'I expect we do,' Dallas replied, puffing his chest out in an attempt to feel authoritative, but it was a hollow gesture. Inside, he knew that, and it wasn't a sensation he could fake.

'Well, don't keep me waiting,' the voice of the Architect said, licking its cadence around Dallas's head. He tracked it side to side, the sound dancing from one ear to the other. Dallas shook his head.

'Alright,' he wheezed, taking the first step up onto the remaining flight of stairs. 'I'm coming. And we sort this out, once and for all.'

Although he couldn't see it, the Architect smiled in his lair. That was precisely his intention, as Dallas made the final climb.

'Hello?' Dallas called as he pulled himself out of the clandestine little stairway and into the Penthouse. There was no answer. Dallas continued, wrapping around past the curtain-glass windows that were stained with time.

He was in the doorway a square room, totally dark. The light flicked on with Dallas' touch. He was back in Chivron's office. He paced around the desk. Some of the books from above had moved to the desk and lay open. Dallas laughed, glancing at black-and-white photos of angular concrete blocks. They cried out for the sort of reinvention this place had gotten, and what this penthouse suite needed.

Leaving the office, he saw a figure in the lounge, which had been empty.

Now it wasn't.

'Who the hell are you?'

The Architect sat in the lower couch area, gazing out across the city. His form fell into total silhouette. 'Good trip? I see you've visited my office.'

'You're him, aren't you?'

The figure chuckled.

'Don't even start,' Dallas said. Then his head glanced around. 'You know what, this whole place could be gutted and modernised. Another five-hundred-grand for the exclusive penthouse. Stunning city vistas,' he continued, gesturing with a wide wave, pushing the air away in a flutter.

'I live here,' the Architect mumbled. 'And your designs mean nothing.'

'Sorry? Did you say anything?' Dallas said. He took his coat off, throwing it over the back of one of the old chairs. 'I don't know what you are. No, wait. I do. You're nothing. Some sort of trick. But you're not really anything worth worrying about.'

'Is that so? Come, sit, join me. I want to discuss my... *our* plans for the Tower's future. See me for who I am.'

Dallas did, moving slowly toward the figure perched in the corner. Finally, the light falling through the filthy window, he saw the bony, gaunt figure comprised of pallid flesh.

'What the hell are you?' The figure turned its head. Dallas reeled. The sunken features were pits of blackness and rot. 'Christ almighty.'

'This is who I am. Supported by the Tower.'

'I saw you've been looking up some more relics.'

'Those *relics* are the future, and you can't contain the concrete form. The future of the Tower is-'

Dallas held up a hand, partly dismissively, partly to obscure the Architect's form from view. 'Look, the Tower has a future. I've planned it all out. You - whatever you are - isn't included in those plans.' The Architect laughed at Dallas. 'What's so funny?'

'You say all this about grand plans, but I know the reality.'

'I could have a team here next week, they'd gut this place-'

'Your *team* are cowboys. And so are you.'

'Those are mighty accusations,' Dallas said. 'For a dead man to make.'

The Architect didn't move. Neither did he turn his head. 'Councillor Grimms is a snake, and you're one too. Your venom threatens the Tower.'

'I don't know what you're talking about.'

'You cheaped out, Mr. Wentworth. And it's all going to come back on you, very soon I expect. You and Grimms have meddled with forces you simply cannot understand.'

Dallas didn't answer for a moment. Then he did: 'You don't know what you're talking about.'

The Architect took his turn to withhold answering. He raised a hand, a finger pointing toward the nearby bureau. A drawer snapped open. 'Look.'

Getting up, Dallas moved over. He glanced down. The drawer was filled with ceramic chips. All were a tarnished aquamarine. He picked some up, feeling the irregular, shattered edges. 'What are these?'

'They are part of the legacy you ordered destroyed. The man responsible paid with his life.'

'What are these from, then?'

'They're from the murals that you deemed gaudy and dated. The ones you didn't just order covered up with some featureless cladding...'

Dallas moved back. 'I ordered those murals destroyed,' he murmured, finishing the sentence. Then he turned his head. 'They couldn't be saved, they just didn't fit in!'

'Everything had its place, Mr. Wentworth. You didn't even do a *sympathetic* restoration of the Tower. You blew away the style and replaced it with a blandness that I find so distasteful. But that blandness is only skin-deep. The true Tower will leech through, back into life.' Dallas laughed. 'The life-force of the residents is where it comes from. Occupants. *Visitors.*'

'Don't you think it's out of proportion, even for you, whatever you are, to kill a man for smashing up some tiles?'

Finally, the Architect leapt from the sofa. 'This, this is the attitude, Mr. Wentworth!' he snarled. 'Such a cavalier attitude toward... toward what mattered most to me! The Tower is more than the sum of its parts, I poured my life and *soul* into it, will you finally attempt to understand?!'

'I've given people nice new homes and renovated an eyesore that had blighted this area for years.'

'No, you did that totally incidentally. You made *money* - dishonestly - from my legacy.'

'Don't you judge me for my success.'

The Architect laughed once. 'We shall see where that success leaves you. I told you when we last spoke, that the Tower was to be truly restored. And you refuse to do that now, even while I know how you got where you are?'

'No,' Dallas said flatly. 'Conjecture from some... student in a Halloween costume.'

'The Tower has filled with bad people. You are privy to this, and you allow it. Bad things will happen to them. And those bad things will be blamed not on me, but on *you.* Your legacy will be as tarnished as you have made mine!'

Dallas shook his head and turned to leave. 'You're insane. I thought bricking you up would be merciful in a way, even if it cost me the four flats on the floor below. But no, I know what you need, you creep.'

'What's that?'

'You need *evicting*. Not just from the Tower, but from this world itself.'

The Architect paused before laughing. The lift door opened. Behind, another hatch opened. A metallic clicking came out of it. 'You first.'

Outside, Scarlett Wentworth reached into her bag for her phone. 'Maybe I was a bit harsh,' she said, to herself as well as George, her friend in the driving seat.

'Whatever babe,' he said, disinterested.

'Can you drop me off at my parents?' she asked. George nodded. Scarlett tapped on her dad's contact icon on her phone and held the device to her ear. Instead of the expected dial tone, however, she got only a steady bleep, like a flatlining heart monitor.

CHAPTER 15

Krystal scurried around, picking items up and not really tidying but moving them. The appearance of being busy helped her forget what had just happened.

She avoided glancing through the door to the hallway, back toward the closed bathroom door.

She looked at her phone. The minutes had swung away. The phone buzzed in her hand, and she nearly threw it out of the window with surprise.

The buzzing was transient, so it was just a notification. She caught the phone as it slipped from her hand.

'Bitch!' she called, responding to the alert. It was nothing - junk mail from a Facebook game. A nail flicked the switch on the side of the phone to 'silent'. Then she looked, realising that she wasn't making any progress. 'Fuck this,' she said to herself and tidiest the worst of the filth with confidence. In twenty minutes the flat was tidier - not great, not like her mum used to keep it, like a show-home, but better. An improvement.

The door knocked. With a gasp, Krystal turned. 'Christ,' she said, clawing over to the front door through the hallway. She pulled on the latch, which clicked. Then the door swung open, the draught excluder rubbing with a swish on the floor.

'Mum,' Krystal spat. 'What are you doing here?'

'Here?' the woman in the doorway said severely. 'Young lady, I think it's about time you and I caught up. Were you expecting someone else?'

Krystal pulled out her phone. She saw a text message:

Dear Ms. Candace, unfortunately I won't be able to make today's in-home assessment. We'll reschedule soon. Ms. C. Evans

'Bitch,' Krystal mouthed, only looking up as her mum brushed past, crossing the threshold.

Krystal's mum Evangeline trotted through to the living room, stopping on the threshold. Her head moved side to side ever so subtly.

'Problem?' Krystal said.

'Not how I'd have kept it,' Evangeline hissed. 'Still, I've seen the places you end up. This is a damn sight better.'

'Thanks, Mum,' she said.

'Almost too much better.'

'Oh, here we go...'

'Shush,' Evangeline said. 'Let's... not worry about that.'

An eerie silence fell between the two women, Krystal evading her mum's gaze.

The elder woman's face cracked. 'Don't be like that, Krystal. I'll make tea, shall I?'

Krystal sat down as her mum went into the kitchen. The kettle clicked on, then hissed with boiling. Then another click with the bubbling of boiling water. A clink of spoons on china. Evangeline emerged.

'You have a lot of things,' Evangeline said without raising her head. 'I'm surprised.'

'Why?'

'You're living alone?'

'Yeah,' she said. 'I am.'

'So,' Evangeline indicated with the end of her spoon. 'The things?'

'Not mine.'

'I see.'

'And some friends have put some stuff in here.'

'That's very generous of you, isn't it?'

'I think so, yeah. If you can't help out your mates when they need it, who's going to help you whenever you need it.' Evangeline said nothing. 'Mum, come on, how did you find out I was living here?'

'Oh, this and that,' Evangeline said. 'We miss you, you know. Your dad, your brother, auntie and uncle...'

'Stop,' Krystal said.

'We can help you, you know.'

'No, I don't need help from anyone.'

Evangeline ducked toward Krystal. 'Is he here? Is this his stuff?'

'I don't know who you're talking about.'

'You do. Don't lie to me.'

Krystal sat button-mouthed on the sofa. Slowly her head turned, meeting her mum's glance.

'What happened to your nose?' Krystal's lip wavered. 'Was it Tyrone? TJ?' Krystal's lip wavered, just a touch.

'I knew it,' Evangeline said. 'This is all his gear isn't it? Probably stolen.'

'Yep.'

'He's bad, Krystal. And not just...'

'How?'

'Your Auntie Eliza, she found out some stuff. It doesn't matter how, it's what we know. He's a lowlife, he needs putting in prison. *Or worse.*'

Krystal's eyes darted toward the bathroom. 'Mum, he could be back any minute-'

'He's done this to so many young, stupid girls.'

'Mum!'

'But they are! But it's not their fault, they get taken in and-'

'Doing?'

'Stolen goods. Who needs that many PlayStations? Check. Those letters,' Evangeline said, pointing to a rough pile of torn-open brown envelopes. The Department for Work and Pensions lettering was enough. 'Benefits cheats. He's setting you up. But he's not clever enough.'

'Mum!'

'When's he coming back? I lied. They've though this was fishy for months. They think I can get you to be the one to send him down. Put an end to this. *Bring you home.*'

Krystal trembled. 'I... I'm not sure if I can, Mum...'

Evangeline held out a hand, meeting her daughter's. She gripped it hard.

'Come home, Christine.'

Krystal gulped at hearing her *real* name. She looked to the floor, through the dust. Then she looked up, into her mum's eyes.

'I'll come home.' She glanced through dewy eyes toward the bathroom. 'This place just creeps me out.'

'Now?'

'No, but I'll be gone before he comes back. He'll never see me again.'

Evangeline smiled, and mother and daughter finally embraced.

Out of the corner of her eye, during the embrace, Krystal looked past into the hallway.

Drops of water seeped from underneath the bathroom door to form a puddle.

CHAPTER 16

'Partha!' Mrs. Choudhury called, just as the front door to flat forty-three clicked closed. She laughed. 'Never mind then.' She moved back to the sofa, perching herself on the edge of the cushion. 'Oh, god,' she winced, grasping at her side. The old lady extended her hand toward a glass of water on the coffee table in front of the sofa. Her fingers wrapped around the glass, picking it up. The water inside trembled against the translucent sides as her grip wavered.

She took a sip. The water was stale, warm and unsatisfying. Holding the glass in one hand, she then reached for the open packet of painkillers that was on the table. Popping one out of the blister-pack, she placed it at the back of her mouth and took another sip of the water.

Mrs. Choudhury swallowed the pill with a gulp.

It hadn't taken long for the Choudhurys to make the brand new flat feel older and lived in. Coloured beads hung in the living room doorway, and family photographs and pieces of artwork covered the walls. Most of these were scraps, taken from place to place, but they all made whatever house the couple lived in feel like a home. These were the accoutrements of decades of life distilled into a miniature mausoleum to a couple who'd seen the world pass by under their feet. Now, in the twilight of their lives, the couple could reminisce without even putting slippers on.

Mrs. Choudhury sunk into sagging cushion of the sofa. She

tugged on a blanket that lay atop the sofa, pulling it over her shoulders.

Something always made her cold. The shiver ran down her spine from tip to toe. She closed her eyes, imagining places warmer to stoke the inner fire of her body.

Antigua, 1991.

India, 1988

Egypt, 1976.

Photographs from all these expeditions covered the bare, impersonal white walls. The imagery seeped from those images encased in cellulose and plastic back into the old lady's mind.

'No, no...' she started moaning. The images dissolved in front of her eyes. Swirling colours took precedence, dominating her vision. 'Not again, please,' she moaned, louder and clearer than before. She swatted her arms to dispel the swirling colours and bring back the memories.

It wasn't working. She winced, squeezing her eyes shut, willing the memories into clarity in front of her eyes

Her and Partha riding a camel. Being stuck in the torrential rain. Vising the family – all twenty-something of them – and trying to recall their names.

The names didn't come. The swirling colours turned into a deep, rippling crimson. The colours solidified into a valley formed of red sandstone against a jet black night. Maybe even space itself. Then, above the valley, two eyes – sinister, sneering yellow things. They were ugly, and they stared past the valley of sandstone, right into the core past Mrs. Choudhury's eyes.

Into her soul.

They saw past her façade, into what she really was.

She opened her eyes. 'Begone!'

'No,' a voice licked into her ears.

She looked about the living room, eyes darting. 'Where are you? You're near, aren't you.'

'Dare you come to find me, weak woman.'

Mrs. Choudhury smiled, getting to her feet. She didn't tremble now. 'You know what I am. That glimpse was enough.'

'What you are,' the voice continued, 'is of no concern to me. I can use your life-force to my own will. Like this-'

Mrs. Choudhury screamed once, clutching her chest. She fell around the coffee table to the rug on the floor. She scrabbled, pulling herself toward a stand just under the lounge window. On it an ornament – a metal figure with many limbs dancing in a ring of individual, stylised torches.

'Oh no,' the voice said into her ear – into her *soul*. 'That ornament won't save you.'

Mrs. Choudhury peeled her eyes open. She smiled, against the force that seemed to constrict her. 'The ornament won't. But the force it represents will.'

Grasping the white doily that dangled over the edge of the table, she tugged. The metal ornament teetered, then toppled to the floor with a thud. Mrs. Choudhury gasped for what she really wanted – the chain draped over the figure. The gold links were smooth in her grip. Then she found the shaped, smooth metal at the end – an amulet.

She then chanted words that only she understood, her lips hardly moving.

A wind picked up from around her, pushing against the fittings of the living room. Pictures danced on their little strings against the hooks embedded into the wall. The rugs slapped up from the laminate floor.

The photos vibrated, then took off, flinging around the room. Some hit the wall, smashing. Fragments of frame tumbled in the tempest.

'Begone, foul monster, I command it!' Mrs. Choudhury growled. She raised a hand from her prone position, pointing to the ceiling. A force propelled her to her feet, for her arms didn't. 'Leave this land and reality, or so be it now that I will cast you out myself, harnessing the -' she stopped.

119

The front door jangled. Mechanism clicked. Someone was opening the door.

'Ha!' the voice in her ear laughed. 'Care to reveal your real self to them?'

'Begone!' she swatted again. The wind in the living room died, and she fell to her prone position, the mess falling to the ground around her.

'Mum,' a voice called. It was Rajat, her son. He stepped into the living room, still transfixed by his smartphone. 'I saw Dad downstairs, he asked me to-'

'Son,' she wheezed.

'Mum, what the hell happened here?' he said, bending down. Mrs. Choudhury held her back, wincing as he helped her up.

'What, dear son, are you doing here?' she asked.

'Me first, mum,' Rajat said.

'No, *me first*,' she said. Rajat gulped. She inhaled audibly. 'What have you been smoking? Again?!'

'Mum, look,' Rajat said, holding his hands up and backing away. 'It's just a bit that Yanis and Kai-'

'You're cavorting with those fiends from downstairs?! Again?! After what they did to your father-'

'Whoa, whoa! That was, like, a one-off thing, they said they'd never do that again, you've gotta believe me.'

'Like you believed them?!' Mrs. Choudhury shouted. She coughed. Rajat closed in, extending an arm to support her. 'Go away! I just need to sit down for a moment.'

'Mum...' Rajat started. 'Look, I'm sorry, alright.'

Mrs. Choudhury grasped for her glass of water from before. She took a large, audible gulp. 'You always say this, Rajat. But you continue to *do* these things. Can't you see these are bad people.'

'Hey, sorry I can't be as perfect as you want to be!'

'It's always the same though! We brought you up, your father and I, to be such a good boy. A better boy. And this is how you repay us. Those fiends, they're not your friends...' she began.

Rajat rolled his eyes. 'Don't you dare!' she snapped. 'It'll be the death of you, or all of us.'

'Now you're just being silly,' he said.

She didn't respond. She broke off looking at him. 'Well, at least you could help clear up. You know how your father likes a tidy house.'

Rajat walked over, picking up the pictures that had flown off the walls. 'What happened in here, Mum? Like you had a tornado go off right in this room.'

She took a deep, heavy breath. 'It's... let's just clear these things away.'

Rajat nodded. He started tidying the upset room. He reached for the upset ornament beside the table in the lounge window. Reaching out, he placed the ornament back on its stand. Then he reached for the amulet on its chain which had fallen to the floor. Picking it up, he threw it down again with a yelp. 'That's hot!'

'What? Give it here, now,' Mrs. Choudhury said. 'Quickly.'

Rajat picked it up delicately with his fingertips, holding the chain for only a few moments. It fell into the cupped hands of his mother. She held it close as she withdrew onto the sofa.

'What is that?'

'Something very precious, son,' she said. 'And powerful. To me and everyone here.'

'Mum, you're scaring me.'

She looked up. Rajat flinched backward. Her eyes were golden, glowing with some fantastic energy. 'Son, do the right thing for your mother.'

'Wh-what's that?'

She blinked. The golden glow disappeared. 'Freshen my water, I can't stand it warm.'

CHAPTER 17

Behind Royston, the front door clicked closed. But not his front door. He chuckled, looking into his phone. The landing was completely dark, but the phone gave off enough light to illuminate his face.

The black sack rustled as it touched the floor.

His phone buzzed. Royston quickly swiped on the screen and put it between his shoulder and ear as he picked the black sack up again.

'Surly,' he said. 'Yeah good. Are you going to come up? Yeah that's sweet, man, sweet. This new thing, yeah, it's going real well. Alright, well, call me.'

He hung up and pulled the black sack toward the lift.

Surly's idea had been great. The lift door opened. Royston heaved, entering. The car shuddered on its cables, just a couple of millimetres. The doors closed, the number on the dark front door not visible. The shadow of the large acrylic numbers that signified the floor were, though, visible in the dim gloom.

The Nineteenth Floor disappeared behind the lift doors.

Royston let the bag fall open. The aroma of the product inside wafted in, filling the metal space.

Royston hummed with pleasure. That smell meant only one thing to him: money.

Flat Seventy-one was now empty, but only recently so. The woman who rented it had moved out, Royston's charms having convinced her to leave it to him. It had been a fun distraction, too. His entire operation had doubled in size from his original flat on the Seventh floor to twelve floors up.

The lift glided to a halt on Royston's real floor. Shaking his head, he tied the bin-bag up again. Before the doors opened, he wafted his arms to dispel the scent. No matter, the fresh air would help with that.

The lift opened to another gloomy landing. Royston laughed again, to nobody. His phone provided enough light. The lights rarely worked consistently these days, it was always intermittent.

After that last bit of theatrics with the electrics, Royston didn't complain. The dodgy lights became *one of those things*.

But Royston stopped outside of the lift, dropping the bag. There was a different odour, not pleasant like the one he'd been savouring in the metal car.

This one was dry, carbonised – one of *scorching*.

Quickly, he fumbled with the door and opened it, falling into his flat.

'No, no, no!' he bellowed. The scorching smell was stronger inside the hallway. Below the door in front of him at the end of the hall was light, which was good, but there was also the haze of smoke, which was bad. He flung the living room door open to a burst of intense, dry heat that flung him back.

The entire crop of illegal plants had wilted. Some of the light fixtures hung at lazy angles, where the glue on the stick-on hooks had started to melt.

He looked to the corner of the room, sweat beading on his face. There he saw the bank of air-conditioners, the ribbons on the front grilled laying impotently downward.

'Screw,' he said, wiping his brow. 'Howzat happened? Oh,' he said, seeing the answer to his question: brown scorch-marks surrounded the multi-plug which fed the air-conditioners.

He walked around the ruined plants in their reflective foil tent to the outlet by the window. Royston put out a hand to try to extract the plug from the burnt socket. It crackled as his fingers approached. He withdrew his hand with a squeak, looking behind him into the room. The lights were now pulsing in brightness, glowing from warm white to an unbearable, throbbing luminescence.

'The shit is all this?! Hey!' he called. The lights started progressively wavering across the room as the glue that held the hooks to the ceiling began to melt like dripping cheese. The first lamp fell, pulling the reflective plastic shroud it was piercing with it as it thudded into the wilted plants beneath it. The halogen bulb smashed with a shower of sparks. The apparatus collapsed around Royston. He pushed out and into the hallway, letting the door slam closed behind him.

Trembling, he reached for his phone, stabbing it with a dirty finger.

'Surly? Surly! Get here. Now. Quick. It's all gone to fuck. You'll-you'll see,' he said without breath, pocking the phone once more.

Poking his head around the living room doorway, Royston observed the mess within, and closed the door again. Royston paced around the flat as he waited for help – or so he thought – to arrive.

'Royston?' Surly called as he emerged onto the Seventh floor landing. 'Royston!'

The flat door opened. 'Surly, well done, we've got a-'

'Slow down! Calmly, now,' Surly said, letting himself past Royston into the flat. The door clicked closed. 'Now what's happened?'

'See for yourself,' Royston said, wringing his hands. He nodded toward the living room.

Surly moved swiftly, opening the door. He glanced in for a moment, turned and looked at Royston. The latter stared back like a petrified child.

'How much is salvageable?'

'None in there. There's one sack from upstairs,' Royston nodded to the black bag on the floor.

'Have you checked upstairs?'

'I just came down.'

'I mean, you idiot,' Surly growled, 'since that happened in there?'

Royston shook his head sheepishly.

'Let's go then.'

The pair took the lift up to the Nineteenth Floor. They let themselves into the 'spare' flat that had become their expansion territory. It was completely dark, but for the orange glow of the lights in the living room.

'How many bags you got?' Surly asked.

Royston opened the smaller bedroom. Surly smiled, seeing it was full of large bags, clearly swollen with cannabis.

'That'll do for now, Royston,' Surly said. 'We'll take that tonight.'

'Are you sure?'

Surly didn't answer. He went through to the living room, opening the door. The halogen lights glowed with their dry luminescence.

'Plants are okay,' Royston sighed with relief. 'Hopefully that was an isolated fuck-up downstairs.' He turned back to leave.

Surly grabbed his collar. 'Hopefully for you, you mean. Don't think I, or we, are paying for that 'isolated fuck-up', Royston. Remember where you really rank in this... *organisation*. I am *displeased* by what I have seen.'

'What do you mean?'

'Call me out with this bullshit. You've got a week to get downstairs up and running again. And it's coming out of your dime. And we want a quarter more product, and you're getting a quarter less payment-'

'Hey, hey!'

126

'Shut up, alright,' Surly growled. 'And do as you're told. Something told me setting up in this gaff would be too bloody good to be true.' His eyes wandered to a corner of the room. One of the lamps flickered, strobing off and on. It dimmed the room just enough to be noticeable. 'Say, fix that would you? It might cheer me up and go toward repaying me for the inconvenience.'

Royston hocked in disgust. With a rustle, he moved his bulky frame around the perimeter of the space, around the apparatus. He groaned under his breath, the words running together in a mumble.

'Get on with it, Royston,' Surly said loudly from the other side of the room.

Royston shook his head. 'I ain't no skivvy,' he said.

'What was that?'

'Nothin',' Royston hissed. He tapped the bulb with a stubby finger. The filament glowed. He tapped it again. The filament glowed again, glowing red as his finger approached. He glanced away. Light burst from the bulb. Royston looked. The bulb exploded in a piercing crackle, shards of thin, hot glass erupting into Royston's fat face. He screamed, falling over.

'Holy fuck, help!'

Surly stayed put. Royston tumbled into the plants, pulling on the wires that held the reflective material up. It crumpled and descended upon him, pulling the lights with it. They shattered all around, Royston's frame pulsating. The broken crown of the bulb had lodged into his face. A dirty, sizzling sound came, and the moans of anguish and distress subsided. He was dead, with his eyes still open, staring into the ceiling through tattered, singed holes in the reflective fabric.

Surly turned out of the flat. He held his phone to his ear, arranging clean-up.

Joel Barton woke up. Next to him, Jules was also peacefully asleep. He stretched against the fabric of the duvet, gently brushing his wife's body.

He rubbed his eyes, feeling some shame at having to leave such a comfortable place.

Then he glanced at the digital clock by the bed. It flashed 12:00 on and off.

'Oh no,' Joel yelped, 'it's happened again!'

He looked at his phone. The screen was dead. He limply pressed the power button, greeted by the red sign of no battery.

'What's happened?' Jules yawned, seeing her husband frantically pulling on his underwear, socks and shirt.

'Power went out again overnight, holy shit! You get the kids up, I've got to get to work! What time is it?'

Jules looked at her own phone. 'Nine forty-seven.'

'Fu-' Joel began as the bedroom door opened. '*Fudge*! Come on kids, let's go!'

Jules threw the covers back and, shaking her head, started on compensating for losing track of the time. Again.

That evening, in the kitchen of flat Forty-four, the lights flickered. Joel entered.

'It's happening again,' Jules said.

Joel moved over, positioning himself behind his wife. 'Any luck getting through to that Mr. Wentworth?'

'No answer,' she sighed. The lights flickered again, this time strobing for longer. She shivered, inhaling sharply. 'God!'

'What's the matter?'

'Don't you feel it? Something... something's really not right.'

Joel embraced her from behind, running his hand along the bare part of her arms. Her hands found his. They gripped hard. 'Don't worry,' he said, quietly, into her ear, 'things'll be okay.'

'I hope so, I really do.'

ACT 3
SITTING TENANT

CHAPTER 18

Councillor Grimms walked from his room into the waiting room at the Civic Building. It was empty but for one person.

'Come in, Mike,' Grimms said. 'This way.'

In the office, Mike took a seat in front of Grimms' sturdy desk. 'Councillor,' he hummed.

'Tell me what's happening?'

'There's problems at the Tower.'

'Problems?'

'Big problems. Mainly with the electricity. But the water, sewerage, waste disposal. My team can't keep up.'

'I know,' Grimms said. He tapped a fat paper folder that was on his desk. 'Complaints. Any sign of Dallas at all?'

'Not seen him in weeks.'

'They found his car parked outside Chivron. Unlocked.'

'Police have no idea. Hickorie too. She's distraught. Have you spoken to her?'

Grimms shifted. 'You realise this brings attention our way, do you not? Remember that man of yours who went missing? Another cold case for the boys in blue.'

'I do.'

'Cold cases attract attention. A tenacity of the police to get under the scab. Expose what pus lies underneath. And you realise the rays of light will uncover certain...'

'Irregularities. That we cut corners left right and centre?'

Grimms didn't answer. Mike cast a glimpse out of the window. The form of the Tower loomed in the distance, sticking into the sky. 'We should've torn it down. Started again,' he said. Turning to Grimms, Mike asked: 'When were you last there?'

'I can't recall.'

'Avoid it. Every time my crew repairs something, another issue crops up. Or our repair fails.'

'More bad workmanship?'

'Not at all, it's all too visible to fake. And it's getting worse. Less *patch-up* than painting over massive cracks. I wouldn't live there, not now.'

'Really?'

'Not for one night.'

Grimms joined Mike in gazing out of the office window across asphalt rooftops, inexorably drawn to one feature in the distance.

Chivron Tower.

Joel Barton held the door open as the twins Beth and Ed scampered in one evening. The door clicked behind them. Joel turned, He saw one of the grocery bags sitting on the pavement on the other side of the glazed door. He pushed. The door resisted and didn't open.

'Dad,' Beth said, 'is anything the matter?'

'Oh?' Joel said, looking over. 'Ed, run upstairs with your sister. Your mum's in.'

The kids disappeared. Joel turned to the doorway. He reached into his pocket, fishing out his keys. The lock resisted as he pushed the metal key in, and it didn't turn. It didn't let the key out, either. Joel twisted the key, his fingers turning white from effort. 'Almost,' he grunted, then felt movement. Metal slipped between his fingers. Pulling his hand away, his wry smile disappeared – the key had moved, alright, but the lock hadn't; the bent key now hung limply from the door. With a couple of shoves, it didn't move.

'Shit.'

In his pocket, his phone buzzed. He answered it, glancing his wife's name appearing on the screen.

'I'm coming right up,' he said, hanging up. Leaving the key in the door, he raced toward the lift. He hammered the button. The mechanism groaned. Shaking his head, he ignored the lethargic lift and made for the stairs, pounding up them.

Emerging onto the Twelfth floor landing, he walked straight into flat Forty-four through the open front door.

Jules came out into the hall.

'What's happened?' he asked.

'Come, look.'

Joel followed through into the living room, stopping in the doorway. The entire suspended ceiling had collapsed, falling into a pile of gypsum and plasterboard across the entire suite. Strips of ruined metal that had suspended the ceiling hung down in tatty streamers.

'When did this happen?'

'I was in the bath, the lights went out then I heard this big noise.'

'Christ,' Joel said. 'Christ, christ.' Then he remembered: 'the kids!'

He opened their room to see them sitting on their beds, looking toward the door expectedly.

'Is everything alright Dad?' Ed asked.

'Yes, fine,' Joel replied, pulling the door shut again. It clicked. 'What the hell?'

Making them jump, the door knocked. Both of the Bartons' turned.

'Sorry to make you jump,' Partha Choudhury said meekly. 'I heard a noise...'

'Has something happened in your flat?' Jules asked, walking over and out into the landing. She rubbed her arms with the cold. 'Christ, chilly.'

135

'Yes,' Partha Choudhury continued. 'We've no heat, and it's like a fridge. It's getting colder somehow.'

'Show me,' Jules said, and followed the elderly man into their flat. It was completely dark, just like the landing. 'No power?'

'No.'

'None outside either.' Jules followed into the living room. 'At least your ceiling hasn't come down. Yet.'

'What?'

'Don't worry,' she said. She glanced sideways, seeing Gopi Choudhury shivering under a thick, Persian-style blanket. 'Mrs. Choudhury! You look freezing!' She didn't answer. 'Mrs. Choudhury?'

'She's had a fever for days. I couldn't shift her. I was about to call for help.'

'Jules!' Joel called through the wall.

'Bring her in in a minute,' Jules soothed. 'We still have power, we'll make you a cup of tea.'

Partha Choudhury nodded, and Jules briskly strode back into her flat.

'Who's this?' Jules said, walking into the living room.

'Hi,' the man said. 'I see you're in as much trouble as we are.'

'And you are...' she said, casting a glimpse to Joel.

'Oh,' the man said. 'I don't suppose we've seen much of each other. Henry Durand, couple of floors up.. Say hello, Helene.'

So Joel finally had a name to this man, who he recognised. He was in the Audi TT 'club', above Joel's measly Mondeo.

'Hi,' the woman next to Henry Durand peeped.

'Their flat has a problem, they're wondering-'

'There's an insufferable smell, you see. It's, it's...' he stuttered. 'Well, it's shit. Actual shit.'

'We thought it's something wrong with the plumbing, but it isn't. There's no water.'

Jules hummed. Joel waved. 'Don't be like that Jules! Everyone's having problems, big problems. We've lost the ceiling, the

136

Choudhury's their heating, and now the, er, issues with Henry and Helene.'

'I think some bad forces are at work,' Mr. Choudhury hummed.

'That's silly-'

'Is it? And now my wife is sick, you saw her? She's been saying things, worrying things. Haven't you noticed it, a presence-'

'What are you saying, Mr. Choudhury?' Henry Durand ventured. 'You think-'

'I know, Mr. Durand, yes. And I think you do, too, Mr. Barton. It all comes from one place.'

'And where's that?' Helene Durand spat. 'Some mad magical man on the roof?'

'Whatever's happening, I think it's all coming from the roof. What's there. Have you been up there.'

'Up there?' Henry Durand asked.

'The penthouse is where all this is coming from, I just *know* it.'

With a great thunderclap, the remaining lamps in the room exploded, showering the room with tiny shards of glass. The occupants yelped in the sudden darkness.

Two small figures appeared in the doorway. The twilight shone on their eyes, picking them out in milky discs.

'Dad,' Beth gasped.

'We're hearing it,' Ed continued. 'The music. From upstairs.'

They went outside into the landing. Here the booming incoherence of the music leeched with more clarity.

'What do we do?' Helene Durand said.

From behind the lift came a rattle, the sharpness of the sound echoing like a gunshot.

'What the hell was that?!' Harry Durand hissed.

Joel edged around the lift. Behind was a maintenance cupboard – there was one on every floor. The door sagged. He took a breath. His nose wrinkled. There was something sour hanging in the air. Then he stepped forward, putting a hand out. The door wobbled, then, as his fingers reached the catch, it opened with a clatter.

'Fuck!' Joel swore.

The Durands rounded the corner. Helene shrieked. Henry held a hand to his mouth. 'Oh my god. That's Liz Crombie.'

'You... knew her?' Joel asked.

'She lived opposite us, nice lady...' Helene said, trailing off. 'Now she's here.'

'I haven't gotten hold of Rajat for days,' Mr. Choudhury said. 'You don't think...'

'Shh,' Jules said fast. 'Let's... not think about that.'

At the foot of the cupboard door, slowly oozing a dark liquid, the crumpled form of Liz Crombie.

Behind her, the mottled steel of an old waste disposal chute, the metal puddled with streaks of blood.

CHAPTER 19

The door to flat Fifteen shivered and creaked. A form emerged, heaving at a heavy suitcase.

'Mum,' Krystal said into her phone. 'When can you get here? I've got the last of my stuff. No, I didn't see him. He's gone, Mum, believe me. I don't think I'll ever see him again. Yeah alright. An hour? Bloody Pete for you! Alright,' she finished.

She lugged the case over to the lift and pressed the button. It didn't respond. She sighed., having to lug the case down five floors of stairs. She approached the external doors.

'Weird,' she said, spotting half a broken key in the door. She pushed. It rattled, but didn't open. 'Shit.'

She reached into her pocket and pulled out her phone. *No service.*

Then from *somewhere*, a shriek. Abandoning the case where it was, Krystal made for the stairs, going back up.

'What do you expect we do?' Mr. Choudhury asked above the hubbub in the Barton's living room.

'I don't know,' Joel Barton said.

'But who could be next? You saw what happened - what's been happening? First those rowdy kids, you remember... then that guy upstairs died. The one growing all those drugs,' Mr. Choudhury said. 'We've all seen these things happen and we are just brushing it aside. I don't want to be next, I just want to live on! My wife and I... we came here for retirement, not some sort of house of horrors ordeal!'

The adults nodded. Nobody wished to relive seeing a black private ambulance arrive to cart away the charred remains of Royston.

'Mum,' Beth Barton said. 'We're scared.'

Everyone turned, the little voices breaking the confusion like a hypodermic needle. They saw two ten-year-olds clutching each other in terror.

'Jules,' Joel said, 'go and see to the children, I'll look after the adults.'

Jules quickly moved through the restless crowd and took the children away.

Attention then quickly turned back to Joel, with Mr. Durand stating: 'Do you have a plan, or any ideas on how we get out?'

Joel took a deep breath. 'I think I know what needs to be done, it's something we've all been avoiding.'

'And what's that?' Mr. Durand responded.

'We need to go to the top.'

'Twenty-third floor?' Mrs. Durand said. 'Nobody's been up there since...'

'The Twenty-third floor is just a stepping stone.'

'To what?'

'The Penthouse. Floor Twenty-four.'

'There isn't a floor Twenty-four, we all know that?'

'You doubt now that what we're saying is true? I've been there, I know what I saw. And has anyone heard from Mr. Wentworth lately?'

'No,' Mr. Durand said.

'He went up there and never came back up.'

'Maybe he's still up there.'

'That was two weeks ago. Things have broken in that time that shouldn't break for months. Years. Something isn't right and I think it's up there. Whatever it may be.'

'Well,' Mr. Durand said, looking around. 'I still think there must be another way. We need to go down, not up.'

'We tried that,' Mrs. Durand said to him. She nodded at Joel. 'All we saw was a case by the door. It wouldn't open. The fire exits either. We're trapped, and I think it's true what Mr. Barton - Joel - is getting at. Something's keeping us in this Tower, it's picking us off one by one.'

'Thank you,' Joel Barton said. 'I know it won't be easy but I think we need to do it, while we have collective strength in numbers. Basically,' he took a big breath, 'before it's too late.'

The group looked at each other, then quickly avoided each other's gaze. Then, Mr. Choudhury looked up to Joel. 'When do you propose we do this?'

Joel looked across the room. He saw in the doorway his wife with their two children huddled together for warmth, comfort and safety. 'I think we all have to do it tonight. Now. Before morning.'

Joel Barton reached for his coat from the coat hook in the pitch-dark flat. Jules held the flashlight, and he took it so she could put her coat on with muted ruffling sounds.

'You ready?' he asked.

She shrugged. 'I don't know what to expect. Is it... really like that? On the Twenty-third floor?'

He grabbed her hand and squeezed. 'We'll be alright. We'll get out of this. You, me and the twins.'

She smiled in the torchlight and squeezed back. 'I love you.'

He smiled, not needing to reciprocate through words. After a long moment he let her warm hand fall away and reached for the cold metal latch on the front door. It hissed against the draught excluder as the door opened. The Landing outside beckoned, pulling the latent warmth of the flat into the void.

Joel took a step. 'I'll check on the kids.' He opened the door. While he did so, Jules fetched her own jacket. Joel emerged a moment later. 'They're not in there.'

'What?!' Jules gasped. She ran past her husband, peering into the bedroom. Two empty beds greeted her. She turned. 'Outside. Now.'

Joel threw the front door open. 'Kids!' he shouted.

From above, the music started playing. He turned. Jules faced him in the doorway. Behind her, the Durands and Mr. Choudhury.

'They've already gone,' Jules said.

'Then we're going after them. Right now.'

'Right,' Mr. Durand said. He looked to his wife. 'Best get our coats.'

On the Sixteenth floor, Mr. Durand and his wife were waiting, casting a disc of torchlight against the walls of the Landing outside their flat.

'Joel,' Mr Durand said, dressed in a thick parka. The stench of decay rose through the stairwell and leeched around the door to the Landing. 'We're ready. Should we bring anything?'

'I honestly don't know,' Joel said. 'But let's just go.'

Joel pulled the stairwell door open, extinguishing the discussion and the climb began. As soon as the door closed the lights in the stairwell lit up with a thick, electrified click.

'God!' Jules said.

'*Come, Residents, one and all, join the party in the Penthouse! Tonight,*' the Architect's voice boomed, bouncing off the angular walls of the stairwell, '*we host that most famous of events - the celebration of the old becoming new becoming old once again!*'

'Who the hell is that?!' Mr. Durand asked through shielded ears. His hands were clamped to the sides of his head, a pitiful excuse to keep the fuzzy bass of the music out.

'That's him!' Joel urged. 'Let's keep going!'

With each step the music got louder, then the stairs began to weep stagnant and stinking water. It dripped down the stairs

142

leaving silvery, slimy trails on the material.

Everyone dodged the rivulets. With each stair they became more numerous, merging into larger streams that rinsed over the shoes of the group climbing upwards. It stunk.

The Twenty-first floor beckoned, the sticky flow increasing.

'Are you alright, Mr. Choudhury?' Jules asked. She'd noticed that the elder man had to hold onto the handrail, and struggled to keep a footing on the slimy coating that made the concrete stairs waxy and slippery.

'Let's go back,' Mr. Durand said. He ran down the last couple of flights and pushed against the stairwell door. It didn't open. Mr. Durand peered through the frosted glass. 'I think there's people there! Look!'

Joel followed. He tried the door. It didn't open. A couple of people ran forward, smacking the door. Through the frosted glass, Joel and Mr. Durand could see them screaming, yet none of the sound breached the door. The figures slowly disappeared into the blackness of the landing.

Mr. Choudhury wheezed, then shook Jules' off as she tried to comfort him. 'I'm not turning back, we must face this thing, this is just some kind of test.'

'He wants us there, really,' Joel said, 'he's just not making it easy.'

'God,' Mrs. Durand said, 'these shoes were expensive. She turned her head to her husband. 'You did lock up, didn't you?'

He nodded. Jules rolled her eyes at her husband. 'Those people.'

'Priorities, eh.'

'Two more floors, we've got this,' Joel urged, himself as much as the others. 'Come on. Before what happens to them happens to us.'

CHAPTER 20

At the next landing, the door from the stairwell leaked with darkness, pushed aside by an eerie wind. That wind carried a strong, offensive smell that wrinkled noses with each gust.

Mr. Durand approached the door, pushing it open just enough to let a column of light escape from the stairwell and illuminate the landing.

'Don't,' Joel warned. 'Whatever's out there, let's just-'

But Mr. Durand didn't heed the warning. Reaching for his torch, he pushed into the Landing. Joel followed, with the others.

'Durand, where are you?' Joel called into the darkness, looking around. He saw a column of dirty torchlight disappear through an open front door. 'Shit!'

Joel trotted after him, followed by Jules, Mrs. Durand and Mr. Choudhury. They all stopped on the threshold to flat seventy-three. The doorway was festooned in dried grime that was dark maroon and viscous. Lumps of it were sliding down the walls.

'Mr. Barton? Mr. Durand?' Mr. Choudhury called, entering the flat. His feet squelched on a carpet sodden with liquid. He looked back up, wanting to pay it no more heed. 'What happened in here?'

No answer. The elderly man trudged forward into the living room. This room had a more powerful scent of decay. The windows were blotchy with effluent mess. He took another few steps, around the furnishings. Everything shimmered with a milky iridescence. He glanced left, toward the portal that led to the kitchen, as it did in all the other flats below.

The kitchen was totally dark, but through the gloom were two figures, shuffling. The old man's breath stopped itself in his throat. The figures moved! Then, trying to turn, two discs of torchlight swung around from the figures and fell onto Mr. Choudhury's chest, illuminating the olive jumper he wore. Then the discs moved, illuminating two faces...

'Good God!' Mr. Choudhury yelped, flinching back. 'What the hell do you think you're playing at, you two! You almost killed me.'

The two figures - Joel and Mr. Durand - looked at each other. They didn't say anything.

'What's in there?' Mr. Choudhury hissed, moving forward.

'Wait, Mr. Choudhury,' Joel Barton warned as the old man approached, but he didn't stop. Mr. Choudhury stopped on the kitchen threshold and looked left. A panel from the wall that faced the void between the kitchen and the rest of the flat lay on the floor. On the kitchen counter, surrounded by dried liquid, a figure lay on the counter, its head disappearing into the wall itself.

'What is that?' Mr. Choudhury asked aloud. He pulled on the prone figure's legs, and the figure shifted, to the surprise of them all. With a wet thud, the figure fell from the counter into a heap on the floor.

Joel's torchlight examined the figure and it trembled, with disbelief.

The figure had no head, just a dirty mass of torn skin and sheared-off bone where a head *should've* been.

Nobody spoke. Joel's torch then danced upward from macerated neck of the unfortunate resident toward the black void in the wall.

Beyond the torn panelling and gypsum board a tarnished metal hatch covered in the sticky substance that coated the flat peeked out. Viscera was caked onto it. Now it was obvious what that pungent, arresting odour had been. It was blood - and it was blood that covered and caked onto every surface in this flat, especially so the kitchen.

'Looks like some old waste disposal,' Mr. Durand surmised.

'And it looks like he lost his head down it,' Joel finished.

The three men looked to each other.

'We should go, now,' Mr. Choudhury urged, taking a deep breath through his mouth. 'Let's go, now.'

The three of them hurried out of the flat, leaving the door ajar, as they'd found it.

Outside flat seventy-three, the three men met the two women.

'Let's go,' Joel wheezed. He began to lead his wife back toward the stairwell.

'What happened,' Jules asked in a whisper as the torchlight danced with her husband's trembling hands.

'I... I don't want to talk about it,' Joel said. He stopped at the door to the stairwell, holding onto the handle. The door danced in its frame. The others in the party gathered around, with Joel stopping them from entering the stairwell. He addressed everyone: 'Until we sort this, let's go straight up. No more side-tracks. Don't leave the stairwell. We have to keep ourselves safe, ready for,' he said, glancing up to the ceiling. He continued: 'Ready for whatever's waiting for us, up there.'

The group murmured in assent and filed back into the lit stairwell, heading upward again up the sticky stairs.

Jules was the last to follow, grasping for her husband's hand as she led their children into the stairwell. Their two hands met, flesh against flesh, pulling warmth from each other.

'It was bad,' he whispered so only she would hear. 'Horrible.'

'You're trembling,' she stated.

'Yes, I... I'm scared.'

'We all are.'

'I feel I shouldn't be.'

'You're doing the best job you can,' she said, squeezing his hand further. 'So brave.'

'Your parents wouldn't believe it,' he said.

'I don't think they'd believe a lot of this.'

The conversation stopped as Jules and Joel went through into the stairwell, to see the Durands and Mr. Choudhury waiting patiently. The stairwell door closed and the Durands took the first step toward the next floor. The Bartons did too.

But Mr. Choudhury stopped, and it took a few steps for the others to realise.

Mr. Durand turned. 'Come on, Mr. Choudhury,' he said.

The man didn't move, instead he looked wearily down the stairwell. In the wrong direction.

'See him,' Joel said to his wife. She moved downstairs, back to the landing.

'Is there something wrong, Mr. Choudhury?'

'My wife,' he said, looking up. He met his gaze with the ashen face of Mr. Barton and Mr. Durand. 'I've left her alone. Will what happen-'

'Stop,' Mr. Durand said. 'We said-'

'We can't pretend we didn't see what we saw!' Mr. Choudhury replied. He looked to Jules, next to him. 'Oh, that was the worst thing. Of all the things.'

She placed a hand supportively on the elderly man's shoulders. 'I don't know what you saw, and I don't want to know. She's as safe as safe can be, given this horrific state of play,' Jules said, making up the words as she went. She didn't know if they sounded hollow, but they were all she could muster.

'Mr. Choudhury,' Joel continued, 'we need to go on so what happened doesn't happen to your wife. And the children. Which is why we need to do this, two more floors, and, somehow, we can end this. Does that make sense?'

The elderly man looked for a moment or two. His brow

furrowed, and with a look of determination, he saw eye-to-eye with Joel Barton. 'If whatever malevolence caused this threatens her, I'll tear it limb from limb,' he growled, before storming up the stairs to the next floor.

The group didn't stop on any of the other landings, heeding Joel's warning. The Twentieth and Twenty-first floor landing doors rattled, almost inviting investigation. The Architect wanted to demonstrate his supernatural power over those who chose to defile *his* building.

The Twenty-second Floor stairwell rattled with a wintry blast. The wet stairs turned to ice in a flash, the slick liquid taking a milky, satin sheen as it frosted over.

'Christ!' Mr. Durand said, slipping. He tumbled, catching himself on the ice-cold banister. It shivered itself under the sudden strain.

'Quick!' his wife gasped, catching him.

'That was close,' Henry Durand said, pulling himself back up. The rest of the group continued. Glancing up, they saw there were no more stairs leading up after the next landing.

Mr. Choudhury took the first step onto the final flight of stairs toward the Twenty-third floor. As soon as his corduroy-clad foot contacted the slick stair, the music blared from up above. It grew louder with each step he took, and there were only a dozen, up to the last landing, where the door waited.

The door slipped open in its frame, just half an inch. It was goading them upward.

'What's that?!' Jules Barton shouted, the handrail she clung to shook with resonance. 'I thought he wanted us up there, to finally have it out?!'

'This is a test,' her husband Joel shouted back as he climbed, 'a test of what he can really do. He's tormenting us because he can. Because we stayed.'

'Do you really think that?' Mr. Durand yelled.

'You haven't met him, he's... a petty, vindictive man,' Joel said.

'Shush!' Mrs. Durand interjected, 'He can probably hear you, don't anger him or say anything-'

'Look, we've come this far, and we're not going to go without a fight!' Joel retorted.

The door beckoned, and with a shove, it opened, and the group entered the Twenty-third Floor landing, hoping to survive.

The lights were on in the landing, a stark contrast to the other Landings that had hidden their desolation in the non-shifting darkness.

The door clicked closed behind the group. With that click of a latch, the music stopped, replaced with the silence, which in its own way was just as deafening. Then small, subtle sounds emerged from that aural void: the hum of current flowing through fluorescent lights.

'What's happening up here?' Joel mused. He stopped, heart in his mouth. The stairwell door clicked closed again with a sound like a gunshot in the eerie silence.

'Hello,' a voice called.

'Krystal?!' Jules said. 'I didn't think you'd-'

'Well, here I am. You happy?'

'Something bad's going on. Really bad.'

'I tried gettin' out,' Krystal said, 'but some madman busted his key in the door. Then I heard... noises.' She looked around. 'The hell happened up here?!'

'You don't want to know,' Mrs. Durand added.

'I guess,' Jules coughed. 'You're with us, then.'

'I guess I am if I wanna get outta here.'

Joel Barton looked up, seeing dirty diffusers spreading the grim glow from lighting tubes. He then looked down, his eyes passing down the walls. The new cladding had been stripped, peeled off and deposited in piled at the foot of the walls. The original puddled concrete had pushed the cladding away. About halfway down the walls, grime-infused synthetic material peeled away like soggy wallpaper. At the bottom of the walls, it had

150

melted to mush.

The Tower was shedding its modern veneer, reverting back to its old, original visage, as its Architect desired. Rejecting the modern grafts onto the cement flesh.

'Well,' Mr. Durand said over the thrum of the music and the whoosh of the night breeze, 'this is the top. Where is this lair then?'

'Shh,' Joel said. 'Look around. Look what's happening.'

'It's awful,' Mrs. Durand spat. 'Filthy.'

'This must be the process; I don't know how he's doing it-'

'Please,' Mr. Durand said. 'This, this must be the work of..' he stuttered.

Joel turned. 'Look, I understand this is all very scary to you. It scares me too. How do you think,' he gestured, 'my children feel? They're up there! But this isn't right, it's not normal, and if we want to get out of here and see morning, we end it now.'

The lights, on Joel's final syllable, fizzled, the tubes crackling, extinguishing in random patterns for a brief moment.

Another door latch clicked, from behind the group.

The six of them filed into the small, cramped corridor behind the lift. They gasped.

The utility cupboard door had disintegrated into matchwood, and the final staircase awaited.

CHAPTER 21

'Stop there,' the Architect said as the group filed into the penthouse from the clandestine stairway. 'I hope you enjoyed the *entertainment* I laid on for your journey to my domain.'

'What is this place?!' Mr. Durand said, pacing forward.

'Kids!' Jules hectored. No reply.

'This is, like, *proper old*,' Krystal surmised.

'I said stop!' the Architect hissed, but Mr. Durand continued, forward into the main living space of the penthouse. 'It's... it's like a time capsule.'

The Architect finally turned to face the group from his position by the main curtain windows that overlooked the sleeping city. The Penthouse was brightly illuminated, the incandescence burning into the night sky. 'Thank you,' he said, turning, revealing a smile drawn across his face. 'I'm very glad you agree.'

'Christ!' Mrs. Durand said. The Architect stood in full glare of the lights. 'Who the hell are you?!'

The Architect's face fell. 'Well, that's just rude, is it not, Mrs. Durand?'

'How do you know my name?'

'I know all the goings-on in Chivron Tower. I *am* the Tower. The Tower is *me*. And I must, if I may, express my deep, *deep* disappointment with you all.'

'What are you and what have you done?!' Mr Choudhury

hissed. 'I demand you stop this and let us leave, now!'

'Kids!' Jules called again. No reply. Again. 'What've you done with them?'

The Architect stopped, pivoting. 'Ah, Mr. Choudhury. You know, I think you are the only one whose... unfortunate events which are about to occur to, I will regret.'

'Is that a threat?' the old man hissed back. 'I'll stop you.'

'Will you now? Let's see what your son has to say about that, shall we?' The Architect murmured, raising a hand and balling it, before clicking his fingers like the hammer on some huge anvil. The snap cracked across the flat, past the group and into the set of private set of lift doors. They clattered open, and with a thud, a figure fell out, lifeless and gaunt.

It was Partha's son, Rajat, his lips stapled together and his body devoid of life-force. The old man looked, quickly ascertaining the identity and rushed over, collapsing in a heap next to his son's corpse.

'Oh, beloved son,' Mr. Choudhury sobbed meekly. He ran a hand across his son's cold cheek. Then he turned, scornful, toward the Architect.

'This is just like what happened to Liz Crombie,' Joel said. Jules reached out and grabbed his hand.

'You had ample opportunity to leave. Some saw sense, though they took some encouragement. But not you. Or any of you. And that disappoints me. It makes what happens here and now entirely preventable.'

'You bastard,' Mr. Choudhury hissed. The Architect waved a hand dismissively.

'This isn't really why we're all here, now, is it?'

'No,' Joel Barton interjected. 'It really isn't. Sorry, Mr. Choudhury, we can't do much about your son.'

'He was a good son,' Jules added. 'Be proud of him.'

'Dad!' a voice called. From a side room, Beth Pritchard appeared. She ran across the space, hugging her dad's leg.

154

'Beth!' Joel shouted. 'Your brother?'

'I'm here!' Ed shouted, following his sister. 'They were going to-' He saw Rajat's corpse prone on the floor. 'He was going to do that to us.'

'Right, now that the family reunion's happened,' the Architect yawned, 'get on with it then, all of you. The last survivors, I'm impressed.'

Mr. Durand sighed. 'What is it you actually *want* from us? We've put up with your trials, now what?'

'Sadly, there is nothing I want that you can provide me. You omitted to heed my warnings, you stayed in the Tower, and now you must forfeit yourselves for that.'

'What does he mean, Dad?' Beth asked, her face confused at the peculiar words.

'I know what he means,' Joel said with a sneer. 'But let him tell you. In plain English. To a small, innocent child. Tell my *daughter* what you'll do to her.'

'Joel!' Jules urged. He raised a hand, stopping her.

'Fine, young lady,' the Architect said, taking a handful of steps closer. 'You are going to become sitting tenants. Permanently. Your blood will seep into the very concrete the Tower is formed of. And you will become, like me, eternal.'

'Huh?' Beth barked.

'He's going to kill us and make us part of the Tower, somehow,' her brother surmised.

'They're innocent children, for god's sake!' Jules hissed.

'I blame the parents,' the Architect said. 'You've had all the clemency from me that you're going to get. Instead, you stirred up the demon within and fed it. Now, you thought you'd come up here and, what? Bore me into submission? I can't deny you're somewhat succeeding.'

Mr. Durand shot a glance to his wife, then pounced, aiming to tackle the gaunt, grey figure of the Architect. Instead, the remnants of the carpet rippled, tripping him up before he got more than a few feet away. The lights faltered just a couple of times.

'I am the Tower, and the Tower is me,' the Architect lauded. 'So,' he then growled to Mr. Durand, 'You want to be the hero, do you?'

Mr. Durand grunted. The Architect wove a hand in the air. Like a ragdoll, Mr. Durand stood, then elevated a foot from the floor, his hunched shoulders rubbing against the worn wood panelled ceiling. Then, with a flick, he was launched across the open space, landing in a heap in the sunken pit by the two decaying couches.

The Architect turned, waving his hand again. Mr. Durand's prone form rose again. The Architect flicked his other hand, a cupboard in the wall with a louvred door flying open. From within, an ancient, old vacuum cleaner emerged, the plug trailing. The Architect waved his other hand again, and the cable unspooled. The chunky plastic plug at the end of the lead wrapped itself around Mr. Durand..

Mr. Durand struggled to breathe. Those struggles turned into a throaty, heaving gasps for one more breath.

'Do you deny my power now?!' the Architect said in a voice that boomed, filling the penthouse. The turquoise mist rose from him. 'Do you deny the immutable presence I have in this place?'

'What are you doing to my husband?' Mrs. Durand shrieked, running forward toward the arcane figure of the Architect. The Architect, seeing, waved both hands again, his wrists turning unnaturally. The bone should've snapped with the motion – but didn't. Mr. Durand dropped to the floor, back in a heap. The Architect flourished one, lazily waving in a dismissive motion toward the woman. The vacuum cleaner dropped, but the floor attachment on its pole did not. This became horizontal in mid-air. Like a spear it flew through the space, slapping Mrs. Durand in the chest with a thick crunch.

She fell, assuming a heap like her husband, both slowly

scrabbling away. Jules helped them to their feet.

'Christ,' Jules Barton wheezed. 'What a nutter.'

'Shh,' Joel hissed quickly.

'Does anyone else want to be some kind of hero? Have I made my point clear with these?' the Architect said.

'Well, come on then,' Joel urged. 'Or are you going to play with us?'

The Architect smiled. 'Playtime is well and truly over. But I can't deny the urge to toy with you before the final act in this little production.'

Waving both hands, the carpet rippled like a tsunami, toppling the Bartons, Krystal and the elderly Mr. Choudhury.

'Let's get the hell out of here!' Krystal yelped, turning on her front and making for the passageway that led to the stairs.

'Oh, no you don't!' the Architect yelled. The door to the arched stairwell snapped shut, the lock sliding across, barring the door from opening. 'Did you really think I didn't know what *you* did?'

Krystal froze.

'I know, Krystal. I know because I *helped*.'

She turned, slowly, meeting his gaze. 'You... helped?'

'What's all this about?' Mrs. Durand trembled. Joel hushed.

Krystal stepped forward. 'You... you said you *helped*. TJ?'

The Architect winced. 'I... I can't control it. The powers that be...' he hissed, another cloud of teal mist appearing behind him. Noticing, he waved it away. A door somewhere clicked. Footsteps lolloped out. One. Two. One. Two.

A second figure in the dark. Krystal yelped. The figure emerged into the dim light, leaving a trail of aquamarine dust.

'Oh, oh god,' she stammered. She recognised the clothing. It was TJ.

The figure stopped in the middle of the space, waving ever so slightly, adopting the gait of a drunk vagrant.

Then an undulating moaning, puckered with the slapping

157

of lips. The head snapped, razor-sharp, locking eyelines with Krystal.

'You...' it breathed, taking a resolute stomp forward. 'You kill. Me.'

'No, you don't understand,' Krystal yelped, jumping backward. She looked to the others. 'It was me or him! He was... he *is* a monster!'

Another step. Krystal bolted, past the Architect, away from the stairway, toward the grimy wall of glass, overlooking the city beyond.

The figure of TJ stomped forward, getting quicker with each step.

'Make it stop!' she screamed.

TJ's figure lolloped forward, balling a fist. It went back in a thin cloud of the turquoise miasma, then came forward in a swoosh, just missing Krystal, but smashing into the dirty glass. It smashed with a tremendous noise. Blood and gore erupted from TJ's lacerated arm. With some superhuman strength, the arm grabbed the aluminium frame of the window and tore it away.

The wind at this height gusted, whipping through the new opening. Krystal scuttled back over the broken glass and uneven roughness onto the roof.

TJ followed her, pushing her toward the edge of the tower.

Joel ran forward, past the Architect.

'You won't stop it,' the ghoulish figure sighed. Joel shook his head.

TJ pulled from the roof a length of metal conduit. The material groaned, then tore away from the structure. He brandished it, raising it above his head. Kristal cowered against the parapet, her eyes closed, waiting for the impact.

But no impact came. Instead, a confused murmur. She opened her eyes, seeing Joel grappling with the remnants of her errant boyfriend, trying to pull the piece of conduit from its' vice-like grip.

158

'Joel!' Jules yelled from the opening. Her head moved. 'Krystal! Get in, now!'

Krystal scrabbled to her feet, scraping the concrete roof. She bounded in, past Jules.

'Now, Joel!' she called to her husband. He looked over his shoulder, still mid-struggle. He felt the figure of TJ push forward, taking advantage. With a growl of his own, he pushed against TJ, flooring the figure. Then he ran inside.

In the midst of the space, Mrs. Durand helped her husband to her feet. But this didn't last long. The Architect re-emerged from the outside. TJ followed, but the Architect held up a bony arm, as if to hold him back.

'You,' the Architect addressed. 'You have dared to *vandalise* the Tower.'

'Not me, him!' Krystal spat. 'That thing.'

'You must pay reparations, but this time – only *blood* will do! Who first?' the Architect said aloud, to nobody in particular. Across the living space, in the wall of the kitchen, a metal hatch built into the wall, the steel scuffed and worn, rattled. 'Are you hungry?'

'Who are you talking to?' Jules managed.

'This,' he replied, flicking his wrist just slightly. The hatch opened horizontally, revealing a circular metallic opening. Somewhere, deep past that orifice, a mechanical growling emanated. The Architect looked at the opening in the wall. 'Go on, fetch.'

Metallic banging came from inside the wall, working its way quickly upward. Then, emerging from the opening, a three-pronged claw on the end of a dirty rubber cable, burst into the space. The claw danced across the countertop, then launched itself toward the petrified group of residents.

'My pet,' The Architect said. 'Good boy,' the Architect cooed toward the claw. 'Did you see? He's got a taste for blood?'

'What are you talking about?!' Mr. Durand barked.

'Oh, yes, of course. The waste disposal. It took that man's head off, didn't you see? You went into his flat. Well, *you* did first,' the Architect said, casting his glance to Mr. Durand. 'You just couldn't resist, could you? Well, your curiosity gives you first refusal.'

'Waste disposal?!' Jules exclaimed.

'Another feature that Mr. Dallas Wentworth deemed... antiquated. He gave the Tower its insatiable taste for living blood.'

'Monster,' Jules hissed. 'You absolute monster.'

'No,' the Architect insisted, 'that's not fair. I've been waiting, really, hoping you'd resist my pleas for you to leave, and you lived up to those expectations. This is how I will make you one with the Tower. You made your choices by remaining.' The Architect winced, bending in pain. 'I tried to *save you all*, but you didn't *listen!*'

'You're going to feed my kids down some rusty old chute,' Joel said, picking himself up. 'You really have no... no *grace!*'

'But you have no means of stopping me or escaping. Look,' the Architect said, hissing through the pain. Now propping himself back up, he indicated to the doorway, which had bricked itself up.

The group stared at the doorway, seeing the cracked plaster regenerate, covering the wooden door almost perfectly. Then it stopped.

'Wh-' Joel mouthed, just as the doorway exploded with a thundering crash of masonry, sending the group to the floor.

CHAPTER 22

The lights went out with a booming thud, prompting a collective hiss of bated breath through the cloud of splintered wood.

'Who's there?!' the Architect hissed, clicking his fingers. 'Lights!' he shouted. 'Bloody lights, reveal this interloper!'

A click came, but not from the Architect, and the room lit up again with a hum of current.

'Good lord,' Mr. Choudhury gasped first from his prone position. 'Gopi, my love! What are you doing here?'

Surrounded by the splintered remnants of the door, Mrs. Choudhury stood strong and firm. 'Husband,' she mouthed. Her face didn't crack from the stony visage. But her eyes glowed golden like ancient jewels in the gloom.

'Who the devil are you?' the Architect said, swiping away. The claw from the wall pivoted with a trill rattle. Mrs. Choudhury scowled at it, and that was enough to send it fleeting quickly back into the wall, down the tube.

'I,' she said, stepping forward. Her first step gave a crack, but not one of bone but of wood. Mrs. Choudhury looked at the bump in the floor, non-plussed, and disregarded it with a glare. She resumed her glare at the Architect instead. 'I am the light who will banish you, the darkness, from the place, and save those you have trapped here.'

The Architect responded with a single, humourless laugh.

'Some chance, old woman.'

'You reject change,' Mrs. Choudhury said.

'Change is awful. Look at the desecration of this place.'

'No,' Mrs. Choudhury shook her head. 'You are the desecration. For change is necessary. To deny that is denying reality itself.'

'Puny woman,' the Architect laughed. 'I reject that assertion of reality.'

'Then prepare, foul beast, for your ending.'

'Gopi, what's happened to you?' Mr. Choudhury mouthed. She looked sideways, down to him.

'I am the light, don't you see?'

'What light?'

'Of this community. Now hush, this devil must be cast out,' she said, turning back to look upon the Architect. 'And whatever force animated him, begone!'

'Smoke and mirrors, Mrs. Choudhury,' the Architect said. He winced, bunching his shoulders in pain. It passed, and the Architect regained control. 'Your form is weak, yes, I can see that now,' he said, swiping out. The carpet rippled again in a tidal wave of loose pile.

But Mrs. Choudhury swiped too. The Bartons and Mr. Choudhury, with her cresting the wave, rode harmlessly over the carpet.

'Get out, all of you,' Mrs. Choudhury urged to the Bartons and her husband. 'Get out while you can! I can hold off his power,' she said, facing back to her opponent. The panelled walls began to shiver and creak, the boards pinging off one by one, the staples that helped them to the wall shearing off. The boards began to hang in mid-air, folding flat and pointing right at Mrs. Choudhury.

The Architect laughed and pushed forward, both hands splayed. The panels flew like loosed arrows, flying straight toward the old woman. She danced, lifting off the floor itself, as they crashed into the wall behind her.

Battle had commenced between forces too awesome to contemplate.

The Bartons scurried down the stairway, clutching their children close.

'Mum,' Beth cried as the noise of the duel above filled the narrow, claustrophobic stairwell.

Jules hushed. 'We'll be alright, come on.'

'Mr. Choudhury!' Ed yelled. Jules and Joel stopped, looking over and up the taut spiral of the stairs.

'Where is he?' Jules shouted.

'He's not here!' Joel responded.

'Get him!'

Joel ran, leaving his family in the darkness of the stairs, and headed up back toward the maelstrom. Emerging from the stairwell, he saw that the penthouse was ripping itself apart. The Architect and Mrs. Choudhury were using whatever forces outside of the scope of human recognition to tear the very fibre of the building apart, to batter the other with. The carpet was festooned with splinters, and the form of Mr. Choudhury, prone and frozen, was covered too.

Past them the Durands, scrambling past to the passageway down.

Joel edged out of the stairwell, dodging a flailing wall panel as it splintered against the concrete in a cloud of splinters and dust. Whatever *was* Mrs. Choudhury had moved. The Architect had backed away from his previous vantage point.

With a shattering crash, the kitchen cabinets exploded, the doors parting. The contents were flying out, through the doors themselves, leaving shreds of the veneer floating in the cloud.

Mr. Choudhury was close, lying on the floor. Joel fell to his knees and crawled forward. He slapped the old man gently on his cheeks. 'Come on, Mr. Choudhury,' he eased. 'Wake up, time to go.'

Mr. Choudhury gurgled, and his eyes opened. 'What... what's

happening?'

'Come on,' Joel said, gently pulling on the old man. He slid across, toward the stairway. 'Time to go.'

Mr. Choudhury began to move himself, shaking the dust off him. He started to crawl. 'My wife...'

Joel glanced upward. He couldn't see the two duellers from his position but heard evidence of their quarrel. The penthouse was being torn apart. 'She's... we don't have much time, I don't think!'

Mr. Choudhury nodded, and picked himself up to a stoop, and fell into the dark void of the spiral stairway.

Behind him, a crash, louder than the rest of the surrounding chaos, spilled out. He looked up. Mrs. Choudhury fell backwards, impacting the back of the kitchen wall with a crush. She staggered forward, showing the depression in the wall left by the impact, a crater surrounded by cracked cement and rendering.

She glanced sideways, trembling. 'Mr. Barton, quick! I can't-'

Another crash came and more material fell onto the old woman. The kitchen cabinets themselves were formed into missiles and projectiles. From around the corner, the Architect emerged, his clothes torn and revealing pulsating grey flesh. The flesh gave off an ethereal, pearly blue glow.

'Barton!' the Architect yelled. 'Deny my power now, do you?!' Balling his fists, the Architect waved. A slab of the melamine worktop tore itself from the kitchen and tumbled through the air toward Joel.

The lights, dangling, quivered. Then, with an arc of current, the first one directly overheard shattered, sending glass falling through the space like rain.

'Shit!' Joel yelled as the glass rain started impacting. 'Fuck!' he winced, feeling the tinkling turn into stabbing with a thousand tiny knives. The second light on the way to the stairwell trembled overhead, shattering in a loud explosion of electricity and glass. The tiny knives rained down again. Behind came a demonic, throaty laugh. Glancing over his shoulder, Joel saw the looming figure, not of the Architect but of TJ, coming toward him. Joel barrelled into the stairwell and turned, feeling liquid running down his forehead.

The Architect stood, eyes now glowing with that grotesque pearlescence, waving his hands. The loudest crash came now: an entire piece of the concrete ceiling of the penthouse fractured. It revealed the the night sky above, and let in a powerful gale of night air. The slab of concrete turned, pirouetting in mid-air. Then, the dust falling from the ragged edges, it shot toward Joel. He ducked, falling into the stairwell, just as the slab smashed against the wall. The concrete groaned with a dry crack, and dust filled the space, which immediately went pitch black.

CHAPTER 23

Joel emerged with Mr. Choudhury on the Twenty-third Floor landing. 'Come on,' he urged, gasping. 'We have to go. Everyone!'

'You're hurt,' Jules said, dusting down Joel's shoulders. He winced in sharp pain.

'Don't, alright,' he gasped through gritted teeth. Jules looked up, just past his eyeline. Pinpricks of shimmer were visible in his scalp, on his neck, on his shoulders. 'Don't touch me,' he finished.

'That looks bad-'

'Let's get out!' he yelled, pushing outwards.

The group edged into the stairwell door, just as a bright flash followed them through, pushing them through with a cloud of intense heat. Behind them, the flare of the fireball erupted, filling the landing.

'Quick!' Jules cried, pushing the door closed. An envelope of flame leapt around the frame but ventured no further. But the Landing beyond the door, through the frosted glass in the door, glowed with an ominous orange flickering. 'Fire!'

'That's all the encouragement I need!' Mr. Durand yelled, pushing past the group and down the stairwell. 'I'm not staying here to get burned to a bloody crisp!'

'Careful!' Joel called, but found himself following, his feet instinctively carrying him away from the rising heat. Swiping Beth from her feet, he yelled that it was time to go. Jules picked up Ed and they started the descent, as the Tower shook and resonated around them.

Rattling came from upstairs, the lights now flickering, hardly able to stay awake. A couple of floors down, the desperate survivors stopped. They turned to face the darkness following them downstairs. Cladding panels melted before their eyes to show the tired concrete behind them. With each step they took, the Tower began its death throes.

One of the modern light fixtures in the ceiling exploded. Everyone jumped. The plastic fixture sagged, dissolving away with the false ceiling like tinfoil. The bulbous form of the original fluorescent fixture coming together in its place like a boil in need of lancing.

'God,' Mr. Choudhury said. 'That's incredible.'

'Whatever power that is, it's horrific,' Joel added. 'I... I can't believe this. It's like a bad dream.'

At the top of the staircase, the lick of orange fire finally broke through.

Mr. Durand grabbed his wife's hand, tugging. 'Come on already! I want to wake up after all this, don't you?'

She resisted. 'Look, though. Have you seen anything like it?'

'What is wrong with you?! Stop gawping and let's get out already, I want to live! Might as well just film it all on your phones, it'd last longer!'

Joel looked down a couple of steps to his neighbour. It clicked. 'Phones!' He raced past, down to the next gap between flights. 'We need phones!'

'I wasn't serious!'

'No, you prat! We need to call for help! Has nobody thought of *that*?!'

Racing down the stairs, Joel burst into the Twelfth floor Landing. 'Holy hell,' he gasped, stepping into the smoke-filled space. The modern, wall cladding had completely dissolved away into pools of melted material at the base of the walls. The concrete that pushed through was dank, festooned with rot and decay. Rivulets of ancient moisture formed macabre barcodes on the pallid surface. Joel stepped forward, feeling the floor move. The tiles were loose on the floor, sliding on what felt like grease. The lights continued to flicker. The flashes of light revealed the dirt and rot - grime and mould - that hugged the regressed concrete.

Joel stepped gingerly into this morass, toward the door that was the threshold to his home. The handle turned, but the door didn't shift.

'Shit,' he cursed.

Mr. Choudhury came over. 'What's the problem?'

Joel kicked the door with a hiss. 'Whatever this is,' he gestured, 'it's locked me out of my own flat.'

Mr. Choudhury tapped on his neighbouring door. It scraped, but opened. 'Come,' he indicated.

Joel followed Mr. Choudhury in to his flat and saw the walls bowing and buckling, the plaster flaking off. Whatever decoration now hung in formless piles at the base of them. 'What do you want from here?'

'Just one thing,' Mr. Choudhury whispered.

Joel followed the elderly man through the ruins of his flat, into the main bedroom. An unmade bed dominated the room, with two ornate, old-fashioned bedside cabinets. Mr. Choudhury scurried over to one, pulling a drawer open with a scrape. His hand rifled through the contents with a delicate tingling, a few seconds later pulling out a chain. Mr. Choudhury's hand obscured the object on the end of it. He then scurried back out of the room as the walls and ceiling contracted with the dark energy of upstairs.

'What's that?' Joel whispered. Mr. Choudhury put a finger to pursed lips, nodding toward the door.

The two men quickly vacated the flat.

Outside the flat, Mr. Choudhury opened his hand, revealing the glint of gold within. A necklace, ornate and formed into a flowing shape, the surface pure and untarnished.

Joel was sure he saw the necklace glint. He blinked. The fleeting glint disappeared.

'From before we married,' he said. 'A trinket. But she always held it close. This has been everywhere we've been. I won't leave it to whatever the hell thing has haunted this place. Though, she usually wears it. Strange.' A low, groaning thud came from up above. Mr. Choudhury looked to the ceiling. 'God, I hope she's...'

'Let's move,' Joel nodded. Mr. Choudhury's eyes closed, and he held the hand with the necklace close to his chest, clutching it to his heart.

'Oh, oh...' Mr. Choudhury moaned. 'Yes, my love, I feel your presence within this...' he trailed off, then his eyes opened like a bolt. 'The door.'

'What?' Jules said. Mr. Choudhury didn't respond, instead he strode over and thrust the necklace onto the lock. A subtle hissing followed, for a couple of seconds, then a click. Mr. Choudhury pushed the door open with a shove.

'Go and get your things, quickly,' he urged. Jules did so, emerging a minute later with the phones and a few random charging leads. She stuffed them into her purse. Joel stuffed them into his pocket. Then the front door to the flat snapped shut.

'What was that?' Jules asked as the group hurried to the stairs.

'My wife,' he said. 'Whatever power she has left, she will guide us out.'

'Cool,' Ed Barton said. Mr. Choudhury stopped, feeling the necklace in his fingers. It emitted a strange warmth into his fingertips. He passed the necklace to Beth Barton.

'She wants you to hold her,' Mr. Choudhury said, kneeling. 'Hold onto her.'

'I will,' Beth said. She grasped the necklace closely.

Somewhere upstairs, a booming thud shook the structure. 'Come on, all of you,' Joel said. 'Before it's too late.'

A couple of floors passed by in a darkened blur.

The descent halted at a wall of rubble that blocked further progress.

'What do we do?!' Mr. Durand wailed. 'There's no way down.' He looked up, seeing the licks of orange creeping along from above, following them down the stairs. 'We're fucked.'

'Hey,' Jules said. 'No, we're not. Don't scare my kids.'

Mr. Durand sighed. 'Aren't they already?!'

'Keep calm, for Christ's sake,' Joel hissed. He looked around. 'Ah.'

'What?' Mr. Durand spat back.

Joel didn't answer, and disappeared out of the stairwell into the Landing. 'Christ!' he exclaimed, stopping right outside the doorway.

There was no Landing, but a chasm three floors tall, the edges ragged, the bottom of the chasm a pile of smoking debris. The open stairwell that led to the lobby – and escape – had collapsed around a void in the floor.

The others peeked over Joel's shoulder. A cloud of dust fell down with another impact from upstairs.

'God,' Mrs. Durand said. 'That's...'

'We're still *fucked*, I tell you!' Durand said again.

'Stop!' Joel shouted. 'Seriously?!'

'That's about a three floor drop. Thirty, forty feet? We'd be killed!'

'Please, Mr. Durand, don't be so bloody dramatic, would you?' Mr. Choudhury admonished. 'Mr. Barton, do you think we could climb down?'

Joel hummed, edging around the ragged hole. 'I think so.' He then started to kneel down and turned, ready to drop.

'Are you mad?!' Durand said. Joel shook his head and felt the edge of the floor slab in his hand. He started to propel himself leftwards, so he was hovering over a precipice. Shuffling, he pulled himself steadily along. Then he winced, quickly, and pulled a hand away. He dangled. The others took a gasp.

'What was that?' Jules called.

'Nothing, something caught my hand,' Joel said, taking grip again. A sharp piece of rebar glistened in the gloom. 'Ah, there you go.'

He dropped down to the next floor in a puff of dust. The pile of rubble below trembled.

'See, no problem. Who's next?'

'Me, me!' Ed called. Joel hummed.

'Let your sister go first.'

'No fair!'

'Do as you're told, young man.'

Ed relented. Beth shifted position. Jules held onto her, lowering herself down so her arms were over the gaping hole.

'Jules, lift her down.'

'Okay,' she said, doing so with some effort. Joel caught his daughter and placed her on the floor next to her.

'Now you, Ed.'

'Finally!' Ed said, repeating the action of his sister.

Mrs. Durand then followed, then Mr. Choudhury, though he needed some reassurance. It was just Jules, Krystal and Mr. Durand left.

'You next,' Jules said to Mr. Durand.

'I'm not throwing myself down there!'

'Oh, Henry don't be such a fairy,' Mrs. Durand called up. 'Just do it.'

'I, I...' Mr. Durand trembled. 'I can't.'

'You can,' Jules encouraged. 'We'll get you. Then you're safe.'

'Am I?' Mr. Durand trembled again, but smiled. It was hitting home. 'Yes, perhaps I- *aaaaahhhhhh!*'

Mrs. Durand screamed too, seeing her husband tumble through the hole. Her eyes – and that of everyone else's – were drawn to where Mr. Durand had been.

One of the possessed metal hooks hung in mid-air. It was just like the one from the penthouse. It danced like a proud python ready to pounce and collect its prey.

'Oh god!' Mrs. Durand wailed, her screams warbling in the ruined space.

'Quick, Jules, get down!' Joel called. 'You too, Krystal!'

Jules dropped and dangled over the edge, scrabbling down. The pincer seemed to follow her, nipping at her. Joel grabbed her heels, and got ready to guide the rest of her figure down. He started pulling, letting gravity do the work. Then she screamed. Joel tugged. He felt resistance.

'It's got me!' Jules yelled. Joel saw her arm in the claw's grasp. He pulled on Jules, but the claw held on tighter.

'Mum,' Beth cried. 'No!' Her brother held her.

Jules wriggled. The claw pulled on her arm. She yelled, the strain on her shoulder intense.

Mrs. Durand ran in eccentric circles. She grunted. Then she stopped, kneeling down.

A lump of loose concrete flew threw the air, just past Jules' head. It clanged on the metal claw.

Jules shifted. She smiled. 'Mrs. Durand, yes! Do that again!'

'Do what?' Mrs. Durand said. 'Oh, this?' She grabbed another piece from the mess-laden floor. She lobbed it. It missed the claw. She grabbed another. 'Best out of three...' With a grunt she lobbed the cement boulder up, but again it missed the claw. 'Oh.'

Beth squeaked and held her hand out. A glint of light on the gold fell into Mr. Choudhury's eyes.

'Use the necklace!' he barked.

'What?' Beth said.

'The necklace, little girl! Use it! Give it to your mother!'

'Oh, alright,' she said, her dad lifting her up so she could pass the necklace into Jules' hand.

'It's warm!' Jules called.

'Yes, use it! *Use it!*'

Jules almost shook her head, then realised. She balled the

necklace in her fingers, and forced it into the metal of the claw that had her other arm. It hissed, and the claw retracted as quickly as it had appeared. Jules dropped down to the floor with the others.

Just Krystal remained on the ragged edge of the upper floor. She turned to lift herself down, but stopped, facing away from the hole in the floor.

'Is there a problem?' Jules asked.

Krystal didn't respond, not to her anyway. 'Hello TJ.' The figure in front of her grunted. 'Whassat? You want me, for what I did to you? Look at the state of you. You're worse than the rat you were when you were alive.'

TJ snarled once. Then charged.

Krystal laughed, and dove into the hole. Her boyfriend's reanimated form skidded past the hole.

'Come on,' Joel said. He grasped Jules' hand. 'We're nearly there.' He glanced up through the hole in the floor as howls of *something* echoed from above. They ran along the floor and climbed down the mound of rubble that formed at the base. The floor felt firm at last, without the incessant, non-ending shaking from above. Ahead, the glass walls of the entrance hall. Escape taunted all of those standing there around the ruins of the staircase.

CHAPTER 24

Oh, brilliant!' Mr. Durand exclaimed as his feet hit the solid concrete pad. Just beyond the pile of rubble where the staircase had once been, the glass walls of the lobby beckoned. Next to the door was a case.

'That's mine,' Krystal said,

On the other side of the glass, the night. Bursts of light illuminated the dark sea of asphalt that surrounded the Tower. Mr. Durand jogged, almost running, toward the plate glass. Safety was on the other side of a quarter-inch of glass.

'Careful!' Joel called, but he didn't listen. Mr. Durand ran forward and put an arm out, ready to simply push the door aside. 'It won't be that easy-'

'It is, it is!' Mr. Durand called in celebration, cupping his hand, ready to grasp the handle. His fingers encircled the bar, then they closed making contact.

FFFFFFFZZZZZZTTTTTTT!!!!

Mrs. Durand screamed first. Her husband juddered, still holding on to the door handle. There was an ugly, constant hum – that of electrical current. Writhing, Mr. Durand fell backward with a bang.

Wisps of smoke came from him. Mrs. Durand stood over his charred form. His eyes were open, but he didn't move.

Mr. Durand lay there dead, twitching as the life fused out of him.

'What happened, what are we going to- *he's dead*!' Mrs. Durand wailed. She rose from her knees, and strutted in a frenzy. She turned, pacing toward the door.

'No!' came a cry in unison. 'You'll be killed!'

Mrs. Durand glanced outside at last, then she stopped her flailing.

Joel walked over, quietly. He put a hand on the now-widow's shoulder. 'It's okay.'

'No,' she said, this time quietly, in no more than a mutter. 'Look. Look outside.'

Joel glanced, his mouth falling agog.

The night sky outside was aflame. Sheets of burning material raining down like miniature comets, crashing into the car park. Embers littered the empty space outside with burning flotsam carried by the wind.

'Good lord,' he mouthed.

'How are we going to get out?!' Mrs. Durand trembled.

'I know,' Beth said quietly. No-one responded. 'I said,' she repeated, this time louder, 'I know how!'

They looked around to see Beth stretching her hand out, a golden, shimmering energy from her clasped fingers.

'It's my wife,' Mr. Choudhury said, moving over to the young girl. 'Use it, use it like a key, like upstairs.'

'Okay,' Beth said, treading toward the doors. Her hand jerked forward, propelled by some supernatural magnetism. Her fingers parted. The necklace raced forward, catching on her little finger. She squealed, dragged along the floor as the necklace raced through the air in a trail of the golden energy.'

'Beth!' Jules called.

The necklace danced toward the door handle, which responded in kind. The crackling, aquamarine energy that had despatched Mr. Durand fought back against the golden glow of the necklace - and the power it represented.

Beth freed herself from the necklace's tails, watching the

dance play out.

Above, the concrete structure roared, clouds of dust billowing from everywhere. Hundreds of tons of structure heaved and moved at the behest of some unimaginable power. The lobby ceiling cracked, plaster and cladding tumbling from the fittings as the old concrete grew back, then bulged up and down.

'There's not much time,' Joel said, huddling with his family just beyond the exit door. The necklace - glowing now like some kind of fairy, fought against the ghoulish energy that came from the door itself. It was being chased, steadily, away from the door and back into the heart of the floor, underneath the very core of the Tower.

The lock clicked.

'Yes!' Krystal cheered.

'Now!' Joel called, pulling Jules and Ed with him. He reached for the handle.

'No,' Mrs. Durand called.

'It's okay!' Joel said as his hand touched the handle. He gripped it hard. Nothing happened. The door opened under his pushing. The sound of the wind outside whipped in and filled the lobby. Joel stepped outside first, followed by Jules and Ed. The bulk of the Tower above jutted out ten feet, sheltering them from the litany of fiery debris that was falling to earth.

'Krystal,' a voice murmured from the centre of the Tower. She turned. There was TJ's ravaged form, emerging from the wreckage of the stairwell. The pile of rubble disappeared, swallowed into a hole opening in the ground. It was from here that TJ had clambered. From the gloom, a mass of twisted metal and crushed concrete peeked.

Other hands grasped for the surface too.

'Oh no,' she said. 'You stay well back. You and your freaky friends you've got coming. You think you can *fuck* with me TJ? With all these magical powers you've somehow got?'

'You gave them to me. And now you give her to me.' He

pointed as Krystal looked, puzzled. 'The girl.'

Krystal looked around, then saw Beth Barton. She clutched the necklace. She looked back to TJ. The terrified visage on Beth's face was enough. 'You can't have her.'

In a booming voice, TJ cast aside whole lumps of concrete that in any normal state would be beyond the strength of a man to lift. 'You will both be sacrificed if you do not yield the girl!'

Beth joined Krystal and held her hand.

'Don't worry babe,' she said, sneering toward what used to be her boyfriend. 'He'll not win.'

TJ stepped forward, his mouth erupting in an ugly, bloody smile.

'I'm scared,' Beth said. Krystal gripped her hand tight.

'Don't worry,' she said, stepping forward, back into the building. The gold and teal starbursts of some mystical, unexplainable energy danced around them both. Beth followed. 'We'll make *him* scared. Let's go do that.'

CHAPTER 25

From outside the Tower, Joel bellowed to those still inside. 'Come on, both of you!' Joel called to Mrs. Durand and Mr. Choudhury. 'Out, now! We'll run for it.'

The two remaining adults paced out, the door slamming shut behind them.

'Where's Beth?' Ed asked over the din. Jules caught the words and didn't react. She looked to Joel.

'Oh my god,' Joel yelled. He looked back, into the blacked lobby. Strobes of energy - gold and turquoise, danced around the space.

And there was Beth, on the other side of the door. And Krystal. Beyond them, the zombie form of her former lover.

Joel ran back, banging on the glass. It vibrated but didn't give way.

'Beth! Beth!' he shouted. 'Try the door.'

Beth turned, breaking from Krystal's grip. A glint of gold chain came from Krystal's balled fist. Krystal turned, nodding at Beth. Then she turned and ran toward TJ in the darkness. Beth ran to the door. It didn't open. The dancing spheres and bolts of energy behind her approached, getting nearer.

'I can't!' she mouthed, her words inaudible to Joel on the other side of the glass. The wind and the sound of the Tower tearing itself apart above drowned out the young girl's cries.

Joel looked past his daughter for a split second. The bolts of aquamarine enveloped the golden sphere and Krystal herself. The gold rays tried to fight against it, pushing outwards in strobes of golden glow. The turquoise bolts of the Architect's phantom energy came from all around. Manifested in TJ's reanimated corpse, the two figures and the forces they represented clashed. The explosion of sparks and sparkles lit up the ruined Lobby like a firework display.

From the maw of this energy, an angular form snared out and approached Beth. It was the metal claw from before. She screamed; her cry inaudible to Joel. The claw grabbed her. She dropped, screaming again, and the claw dragged her into the dark abyss in the centre of the lobby.

'No, god!' Joel yelled, pounding his fists on the glass. It was steadfast and wouldn't budge. 'Beth! Come back!'

Mr. Choudhury placed a hand on his shoulder. 'Come on.'

'I'm not leaving my beautiful daughter in-'

'Think of your wife and your son! We have to move! Now! The Tower's collapsing!'

Joel turned, his eyes dewy. Jules and Ed huddled together by Mrs. Durand. He glanced one more time at the empty space where Beth had been. Then he turned and walked back to his wife.

'Where's Beth?' she asked. He didn't answer, instead pushing her away from the Tower, into the open air. 'Joel. I said, where's Beth?'

'I-'

Where is our daughter?!'

He didn't answer. What could he say? But he hurried, the four survivors running across the car park. Streaks of fire and flaming material rained down around them. At the edge of the car park they turned, watching the Tower burn and melt, like a gigantic candle, with a bright orange flame that shot into the sky forty feet. The walls fell slowly in on the hollow, wrecked middle.

Sparkles of gold and aquamarine blue came from the smashed

180

windows. The entire Tower shook, the concrete splintering like brittle glass.

'It's going!' Mr. Choudhury said over the din. 'Look at that.'

The flames exploded in a final, massive column that enveloped the Tower in a gigantic ball of flame. A roar followed that spread through the night as the Tower finally gave up and heaved one last time. The external walls bowed like wet cardboard, then smashed down to the car park below.

Joel, Jules, Ed and the other residents covered their faces. The cloud of dust from the collapse swooshed across the car park.

Then the quiet came.

'Joel,' Jules ventured. She reached out, grasping his hand. It was clammy but welcomed the grip, reciprocating

'Oh, Jules-'

'Joel!' she barked. 'You did everything you could.'

'But she-'

'No. You did what any father would.'

Joel swallowed hard and nodded. Glancing one more time at the site of the Tower, he began the walk down the road and away. Rounding the corner, the blue flashing lights of emergency vehicles filled the road.

A fire engine stopped just in front of the group. The crew alighted, the commander holding his white helmet under his arm.

'You took your time!' Mrs. Durand said.

'The roads, everywhere, they were blocked. We couldn't get any closer. Not until now.'

'Fat lot of good that does us.'

'The Tower?' the commander asked.

'Gone,' Mr. Choudhury said.

'I see. Are you the only-'

'Yes.' Mr. Choudhury finished. 'We're the only ones who made it out alive.'

'Right then, we'd better get you four away,' the commander

said, leading the survivors to a convoy of police cars and ambulances that lined the street.

Every house had its windows open, the occupants hanging out to get a glimpse. The survivors felt every eyeball on them, like walking down a macabre catwalk on full display.

Climbing into the first ambulance, Jules and Joel held onto their son.

'Where's Beth,' Ed asked innocently. 'She's missing out on this ride in the ambulance.'

Jules gave a look to Joel, out of sight of the young boy.

'She's wherever you are now, son,' Joel said, holding his son close into his chest. 'She'll always be watching over you. She'll be your guardian angel.'

EPILOGUE

Sandy Grimms glanced out of the Civic Building window as he shoved his belongings into a cardboard box. It was evening, twilight, and he had a train to catch.

Down the hall, doors opened and closed. After the disaster at Chivron Tower, Sandy wasn't the only one planning on getting the hell out of Dodge.

'Shit!' he gasped, looking at his watch. He flung a few more sentimental trinkets from the desk into the box and threw the lid atop it. Picking it up, he bashed out of the room, leaving the door swinging.

He hurried toward the lift. He'd been told to prepare for this, but hoped it'd never happen. The box fell from his arms, thudding to the ground. 'Fuck!' Sandy swore, picking up the now-dented box. Looking up, he was sure he saw a shadow sweep around the corridor in front of him.

Turning the corner himself, he paused. The display on the wall of current Borough councillors was just next to the lift. He passed it without even looking, past a load of dusty photographs.

Pressing the lift button, he gazed, just for a moment. Dignitaries all photographed here, some going back years, to when the Offices opened in 1972.

The lift door opened with a clatter. Sandy entered, walking past one last photograph.

Architect, Herve Chivron, proudly presents the Borough Mayor, pictured, with the key to the newly-finished Civic Building, designed by Mr. Chivron. He is pictured in front of his grand plan for the Borough, an estate centred around a monumental new tower block, Chivron Tower.

As the lift doors closed, Grimms glanced the photograph. He smiled inanely, then the form of the model behind him came into clarity.

But it was too late. The lift doors closed.

The floor indictor glowed red, illuminating the letter B.

Nobody heard Councillor Grimms scream...

The throaty rattle of a diesel engine propelled the Transit van through the streets toward the site. It idled outside the gate. Beyond the gate, the site of Chivron Tower, now a gaping chasm in the ground filled with rubble and remnants.

Two doors clicked open and closed. The chain on the gate rattled, and the gate squealed open.

The van moved slowly in, the tyres scrabbling against the loose stone.

It stopped, the engine dying in a whimper.

The doors opened. The occupants moved to the back of the van, opening the doors. With a heave of effort, they pulled the cargo out one at a time. Black polythene-wrapped objects, just under five feet long and a couple feet across.

One contained the Mayor. Another contained Sandy Grimms.

The trench beckoned, and with a damp thud, the packages hit the bottom. They joined the rest of the rubbish – steel, cement, carpet and bone.

Another motor started. Shovels of sand and cement were thrown into the drum with a few buckets of water.

The cement poured into the bottom of the trench, covering the objects, and the van drove away into the night.

Whatever happened to the site, it would always now be a graveyard.

ACKNOWLEDGEMENTS

I'd firstly like to thank my beta-readers and ARC readers for their time, effort and feedback, all of which has been an inimitable help in the shaping of *Nightmare Tenant*: **Victoria Wren, Bethany Votaw, Cheryl Bennet, Dan Hook, Kent Shawn, Hannah Palmer, Colin Clark** and **Charlotte Dodd**.

To my friend **Chris Kenny**, whose companionship and inspiration on a daily basis has helped me reach for new heights. To **Martin Lejeune**, too, for his sage and wise counsel throughout the design process.

To all those on the Author Pals Discord server, and those friends across social media; your companionship, support and camaraderie has been incredible. *Nightmare Tenant* was written during a truly awful time for the world (during the coronavirus pandemic) and your presence has been a great positive factor that I hugely appreciate.

And, finally, to the reader for picking my little story and giving it a go. For getting this far; I hope you enjoyed it! Keep an eye for more my work, as you ain't seen nothin' yet!

ABOUT THE AUTHOR

Richard Holliday is an author from London. He graduated in 2018 with a degree in Creative Writing with English Literature from Kingston University. He has been writing since a young age, initially with an interest in science-fiction, but is also emerging into the horror and thriller genres. He lives with two cats.

Discover more of Richard's work and sign up to his newsletter at
richardholliday.co.uk

Printed in Great Britain
by Amazon

59855967R00113